{catalyst

Novels by Laurie Halse Anderson

*Speak*

*Fever 1793*

*Catalyst*

# {catalyst

## LAURIE HALSE ANDERSON

**VIKING**

VIKING

Published by the Penguin Group

Penguin Putnam Books for Young Readers,

345 Hudson Street, New York, New York 10014, U.S.A.

Penguin Books Ltd, 80 Strand, London WC2R 0RL, England

Penguin Books Australia Ltd, Ringwood, Victoria, Australia

Penguin Books Canada Ltd, 10 Alcorn Avenue, Toronto, Ontario, Canada M4V 3B2

Penguin Books (N.Z.) Ltd, 182-190 Wairau Road, Auckland 10, New Zealand

Penguin Books Ltd, Registered Offices: Harmondsworth, Middlesex, England

Published in 2002 by Viking, a division of Penguin Putnam Books for Young Readers.

10  9  8  7  6  5  4  3  2  1

LIBRARY OF CONGRESS CATALOGING-IN-PUBLICATION DATA

Anderson, Laurie Halse.
Catalyst / by Laurie Halse Anderson.
p. cm.
Summary: Eighteen-year-old Kate, who sometimes chafes at being a preacher's
daughter, finds herself losing control in her senior year as she faces difficult neighbors and the possibility that she may not be accepted by the college of her choice.
ISBN 0-670-03566-1 (hardcover)
[1. High schools—Fiction. 2. Schools—Fiction. 3. Neighborliness—Fiction.
4. Death—Fiction. 5. Fathers and daughters—Fiction.] I. Title.
PZ7.A54385 Cat 2002    [Fic]—dc21    2002007115

Printed in USA
Set in Melior
Book design by Nancy Brennan

This book is dedicated to the memory of
Edith MacDonald Larrabee.

*Take my hand and walk with me in the forest. . . .*

# Part I | **Solid**

$$C_p \, ice = 2.1 \, \frac{J}{g\,^\circ C}$$

"The rate of a chemical reaction depends on the frequency and force of collisions between molecules."

—*ARCO Everything You Need to Score High on AP Chemistry*, 3rd Edition

# 1.0 █ Elemental

*SAFETY TIP: Never carry out unauthorized experiments.*

I like to run at night. No one watches me. No one hears my sneakers slipping in the loose gravel at the side of the road. Gravity doesn't exist. My muscles don't hurt. I float, drift past churches, stores, and schools, past the locked houses and their flicker-blue windows. My mind is quiet and clear.

A ghost hovers off my left shoulder. I can almost hear her breathe. I pick up the pace. She doesn't scare me; I know I'll win. Well, I'm pretty sure I'll win. Chances are good.

On the outside I am Good Kate, Rev. Jack Malone's girl, isn't she sweet, she helps so much with the house, so sad about her mother, and she's smart, too, seen her name in the papers for honor roll this and science fair that, she's got scholarship written all over her, runs pretty fast, she's so good with her brother, why can't all teenagers be like her?

On the inside I am Bad Kate, daughter of no one, she's such a bitch, thinks she's all that, prays with her eyes open, lets her boyfriend put his hands all over her, Miss Perfect, Miss Suck-up, disrespectful, disagreeable, still waters run deep and dirty, she's going to lose it, just you watch, I've seen her type before.

Run faster.

Sweat trickles along the bones of my face and licks my neck. Running, sweating, evaporating... I'm distilling myself in the dark: mixture, substance, compound, element, atom. The ghost is getting closer. Run faster. Push beyond the wall, push beyond my limits. My chest is flayed open; no lungs to breathe with, no heart to pound. The air flows around and between my shiny bones. My skin is silk. I take it off when I get hot.

The first night I ran late like this, the puddles were filmed with ice. Now the trees are leafing and the roads are dry and I fly almost naked, breathless, running out of the empty night into a place where I can't hear myself think.

I wish I never had to stop.

## 1.1 ▌ Stasis

I take a quick shower and pull on old sweats and two pairs of socks. It's only quarter after one and there's no way I'm going to fall asleep, not with all the crap running through my head. But that's a good thing. Insomnia rocks, actually. You can get a lot done if you don't sleep. I've turned into a hyper-efficient windup Kate doll, super Kate, the über-Kate. I wish this had happened last year. It would have given me more time to study for my AP exams.

I head downstairs to finish the laundry. The rest of the family does not share my passion for clean clothes. Dad (age 47; hobbies: religion, football, losing hair) wouldn't notice if he wore the same pair of pants for a month. Toby (age 14; hobbies: trombone, soccer, masturbation) doesn't know how to find the laundry room. I take the clean load out of the dryer, move the wet stuff over, and empty the hamper into the washing machine. I pour in the soap and set the dial to regular.

Bad Kate mutters that they need to start washing their own clothes. What are they going to do when I go to MIT? Good Kate doesn't mind. She thinks there is something soothing about doing the laundry, something de-stressing. Besides, I don't leave for another four months.

Bad Kate points out that I have not been accepted yet. She can be a real bitch after midnight.

I carry the dry clothes to the family room and dump them on the couch. Sophia, our Siamese cat, strolls into the room and hops up on the recliner. She is followed by her boy-toy, Mr. Spock, our black Lab. He lies down in front of her chair with a groan.

I set up the ironing board, plug in the iron, and turn on the TV to the Sci-Fi Channel. A bug-eyed, tentacled alien has just totaled her spaceship in a cornfield. (The ship looks alarmingly like my car.) A SWAT team confronts her in the middle of all that corn. Poor little alien.

I pull one of Dad's shirts out of the pile and iron it. By the time I'm done, it can almost stand up by itself. Nobody irons like me. As I button the shirt on its hanger, a deep, wet cough echoes down the stairwell. Sophia and Mr. Spock stare at me, their black eyes drippy and wide like cartoon animals.

"I gave him his medicine at ten-thirty," I say.

Another cough, as if on cue. Sophia flicks her tail in irritation. I set the shirt hanger on the edge of the ironing board. Toby has allergies, asthma, and a bad cold. It sounds as if he has a quart of pus in his lungs.

"He needs to cough," I remind the cat. "It clears the mucus." I check my watch. Pause. Pause. Toby coughs again. This one is better, productive and short. And then it's quiet. "See?"

Sophia bends over and licks her butt.

"Oh, lovely. Thank you."

I lay another shirt on the ironing board. Toby is fine. Really. I checked his peak flow when he took the medicine, and he was way out of the danger zone. I pull out another shirt and spray starch on the collar. It's not like this could get serious or anything. It's just annoying, all that soggy noise—disgusting.

I set the starch can on the end of the ironing board and pin down the collar with my fingertips. When I skate the hot iron across the cloth, the starch bubbles and hisses. I press the collar, work my way around the buttons, smooth out the buttonholes, and flatten the cuffs. When the detail work is done, I lay the shirt facedown and iron back and forth, back and forth. The wrinkles vanish. Next victim.

On the television, the battle is heating up. The alien burbles something and whips out a weapon (though for all we know it could be a tentacle cleaner). The SWAT team lobs a canister of tear gas at her feet and it explodes. The alien falls to the ground, clawing at her eyeballs.

I stop ironing. That is a major logic flaw: no alien lifeform would be affected by tear gas the way humans are. She's probably not even carbon based. Don't these writers know anything? Geez.

I iron and iron and the movie goes downhill. Dad's shirts and khakis are hung on hangers, his jeans are folded, his T-shirts stacked in his basket with all the limp, dark Dad socks. Sophia is asleep, her nose tucked under her tail. Mr. Spock yawns. I can't help it; I yawn back. Oh yeah, sleep . . . a good concept. But I need to finish Toby's clothes . . . and I should finish tomorrow's to-do list, I should run the dishwasher. I should sleep, I should sleep, I should sleep. I know I should sleep, but knowing and doing are two different beasts. I'm stressed, duh, but it's almost over. The finish line is in sight and I can hear the crowd roaring.

I quickly iron my brother's pants and shirts, keeping half an eye on the movie. They'd be treating that alien nicer if they knew about the mothership idling over Idaho. Just once I'd like to see the aliens win.

Toby's goalie shirt is at the bottom of the pile. You should never iron goalie shirts because they melt. I turn off the iron, unplug it, and move the plug three feet away from the wall. I know it is completely illogical to think that electricity could arc from the socket to the plug and heat the iron and burn the house down, but it's almost two in the morning and I'm feeling a little lightheaded, so better safe than sorry.

The movie breaks for commercials that try to sell me beer, leg hair remover, and steak knives. Oh, wait, one more—the psychic hotline. Gak. Gak. Gak.

Last scene. They have the alien in a hospital hooked up to tubes and monitors. They are transforming her. Human flesh grows and covers her sapphire scales. The tentacles recede, and blonde hair sprouts from her scalp. Eyeballs grow into their sockets. White-coated scientists nod and approve. It's a conspiracy. She's perfect.

Toby coughs again. The cat wakes up and scowls.

I pick up the basket. "I know, I know. I'm going."

## 1.1.1 ▌ Relative Density

My brother's room stinks of male adolescent: used socks, dirty hair, cologne, and rotting fruit. It's too warm in here and wicked humid, ideal breeding conditions for germs. You can practically see bacteria swarming in the air. I turn on the light, perch next to the patient, and poke his shoulder.

"Wake up, Tobe. You need more medicine."

He groans once and flails an arm. Toby looks a little like Dad, I guess. He's got the brown hair, the eyes close together. His face is long and peppered with zits. His ears are finally the right size for his head, but he needs to give up on the mustache-in-training. It looks like a fungal growth.

I shove his shoulder harder and pull back the quilt. He fumbles for it and croaks, "Go away."

I pull the quilt out of reach. "You are coughing up pieces of lung and it's grossing me out. Sit up."

He starts to say something, but a cough strangles him. He clutches the pillow and hacks. When the spasm is over, his fingers relax. I put my hand on his forehead. It's not a precise way to measure a fever, but people are always doing it in commercials. Toby's forehead is oily. I don't think that's related to the cough.

He blinks and sits up, leaning against the headboard. I hand him the plastic cup of green cough medicine. "Drink it."

He gulps it down. "Blech. That's disgusting."

"It's good for you." I pick up a half-finished bottle of Gatorade from the floor, unscrew the top, and hand it to him. "You need to go back to the doctor."

He polishes off the bottle in three gulps and drops it in an ocean of used Kleenex. "No, I don't. It's just allergies. What time is it?"

"Almost two."

"Dang. It's late."

"Duh. Go back to sleep. Your clean clothes are on the dresser. Put them away in the morning."

He nods and pulls the quilt back up to his chin. I toss the empty bottle in the trash and start picking up the tissues that litter the bed and floor. Hiding under the tissues is this month's *Playboy* folded open to a revealing interview with

Miss April. Toby, suddenly awake, sits up again and snatches it away from me.

"Don't say anything," he says.

"Why bother? I don't care. You're programmed to like that crap. You can't help it."

"Shut up."

"Whatever." I carry the trash can to the door. "It's all silicone, you know."

"What is?"

"The breasts, moron. In the pictures. They aren't real. They're pumped with silicone, the same stuff they use to make space suits. Think about that the next time you're, ah, taking care of business."

"Thanks, Kate. I feel much better now."

"Just don't leave it where Dad can find it, okay? We don't need any more fireworks around here."

A car rolls up the driveway and Mr. Spock barks.

"Speak of the devil," Toby says with a yawn.


## 1.2 ▌ Atomic Family

I jog to my room and dive into bed just as the back door opens. Keys clang on the kitchen table, then slide off and drop to the floor. I can hear Dad chuckle. Whatever tragic emergency yanked him out of here at dinnertime must have turned out all right. Maybe he talked a jumper off the ledge, or rescued a small child, or negotiated peace in a faraway country. Maybe he won a poker game.

He turns off the lights in the family room, then climbs the stairs. He passes my room, opens Toby's door . . . quiet pause . . . he closes it. He walks down the hall to his own room, whistling Bach. Another pause. *Click-click.* His door shuts.

Toby and I are the proton and neutron of our atomic family unit. Dad is the loosely bonded electron, negatively charged, zooming around us in his own little shell. From the outside, we seem to fit together perfectly. From the inside, things are different.

Enough. I am going to sleep right now. This minute.

Any second now.

Watch me sleep. . . .

Shoot.

I turn over and punch the pillow. My friends all have tricks for falling asleep. Sara meditates. Mitch recites the presidents, in order. Travis reviews all of his relatives: the stepsiblings, half-sibs, ex-in-law great-aunts, and third cousins twice removed by divorce, then added back by remarriage. (His parents change spouses the way some people change clothes.) Travis rarely has insomnia.

My dad was married only once, to my mom. The marriage broke up when she died nine years ago. I have one brother, some cousins in Australia, and two living grandparents: one in a nursing home and one in a commune. Half a dozen relatives, tops.

Still awake. Stone-cold awake. In a few hours, I will be mixing unstable chemicals near a Bunsen burner. That is not a pretty picture. I'm freezing. I get out of bed, open the closet door, and pull down my old comforter from the top shelf. I spread it over the top of my blankets, then snuggle in. The extra weight feels safe, the satin edge smooth like candy against my cheek.

Still awake. Sigh. Let's try the mantra. *MIT, MIT, let me in, let me in.*

Bad mantra. It makes my heart beat faster and my stomach churn.

Sara doesn't understand why I'm so stressed. I should have told her. I should have told Mitch, too. Maybe even Dad. You know how you're supposed to apply to five or ten or twenty of your top schools and then a couple of safeties Just in Case? Well, I sort of didn't follow the rules. And I sort of neglected to tell anyone. I only filled out one application, to MIT, and I don't sleep anymore.

Sara sleeps fine because she's Bryn Mawr early decision and has a hefty financial aid package. She thinks I should be positive, not fractured crazy, that I should breathe and visualize happy thoughts. Happy thoughts, happy thoughts. Massachusetts Institute of Technology. My home planet. My people. Visualize opening the envelope: "We are pleased to inform you . . ." Visualize jogging on the Cambridge campus, visualize the chem lab, my goggles, my perfectly starched, size four lab coat.

They will let me in. They have to let me in. There is no option.

An owl hoots and I peek out the window beside my bed. The moon is up, but it's not throwing much light. The cemetery behind our house is dark. Beyond the last row of graves, down the hill, down to the stone fence, the air is black. At the bottom of the hill there is a farmhouse, the Litch house, with one light turned on in a second-story window. Teri Litch is either up very late or obscenely early. I doubt she's angsting about college acceptance letters. She's probably planning a bank robbery.

I lie back down and put my arm above my head so I can hear my watch tick. When does night end and morning begin, anyway? Officially, I mean.

Zen questions like that work better than warm milk. I submit and submerge.

# 2.0 | Delayed Reaction

*SAFETY TIP: Store flammable substances appropriately.*

*Bump. Bump. Bump.*

The wall behind my head is being bumped.

*Bumpbumpbumpbump.*

Oh, God. Toby. Are all fourteen-year-old boys like this? If he doesn't give it a rest, his equipment is going to fall off, I swear. I'll never be an aunt.

*Bumpbumpbumpbumpbumpbumpbump.*

At least he's not coughing. And he has enough oxygen for aerobic exercise.

*Bumpbumpbumpbumpbumpbumpbumpbumpbump.*

But there is a time and place for everything. Preferably where I can't hear it. I sit up and pound the wall with my fist. "Knock it off, perv!"

Something crashes.

I smile and pull up the covers. If he's going to whack off before school, he should do it in the shower and clean up afterward.

School.

My eyelids snap open, roller blinds tugged hard and released. What day is it? What time is it? I pull my watch close to my nose. Quarter to seven. Today: chem lab, history quiz, track practice. Crapcrapcrap. I'm late. I'm way late. Sixty minutes late. I've lost an hour. Oh, crap. I hate being late.

I put on my glasses, get out of bed, turn on my computer, and open my closet in one movement. Clothes: black sweater, jeans. Clean underwear, clean, unnecessary bra. (God forgot to give me breasts. Is it any wonder I'm an atheist?) Socks—two pairs. My toes still think it's February.

Sophia noses open my door and slinks in, Mr. Spock close on her heels. My audience. I strip and log on to the Net. My skin is so pale it looks blue, like skim milk. That can't be healthy. I get dressed and toss my dirty stuff in the hamper. My e-mail is mostly stupid jokes forwarded by people who think they know me. *Delete all.* Ms. Cummings sent me a chemistry geek article. Her note says, "It's coming soon— chin up!" And a smiley face.

Good Kate smiles back. Bad Kate taps her watch. We're late, we're late.

I turn to the computer, then spin around to my dresser. *Whoa, dizzy.* Moving too fast. I grip the chair until the room comes back into focus. I swear I am going to drink chamomile tea tonight and try for a normal bedtime.

I pull my hair back in a ponytail, bolt for the door, trip over the dog, and almost smash my face into the wall. Stupid dog.

## 2.1 ▌ Acid

It takes an average of twelve minutes to get out of this house
in the morning. Today I'll do it in five. I dump two cups of
cat food in Mr. Spock's bowl—they can share. I fill the water
bowl from the tap—no, Sophia, I'm not washing it out for
you—and put it on the floor.

I lay out Toby's meds on the counter: a daytime cough
suppressant, two asthma inhalers, multivitamin, extra vitamin C. I used to put out his cereal bowl, but he hates that. I
wish I had time to make him oatmeal. Pop-Tarts, he'll snarf
those in a heartbeat. I pop a couple of vitamin C myself and
drink a glass of orange juice. Once upon a time, when I was
truly the perfect daughter, I used to make breakfast for Dad.
He never ate it.

Enough. Check the calendar. . . . Church dinner tonight,
won't have to cook . . . did I pack my racing shoes? . . . my
contacts come in on Saturday . . . call work, make sure
they're letting out me early . . . allergy doc has to postpone
Toby's shots. Wait—did Mr. Spock get a rabies shot this year?
Why did I think of that, and where did I put my keys?

"Running late?"

The voice startles me. I didn't notice Dad sitting in the
corner, watching me over the top of *The Post-Standard*. The
light above the kitchen table makes the shadows under his
eyes darker than usual. He's wearing an ancient sweater with
a frayed collar over a black turtleneck, and the jeans that I

ironed last night. Meet my father, Rev. Jack Malone, God's public relations guy. The preacher.

"I overslept," I explain.

He turns the page, lays the paper on the table, and smooths it flat. Dissecting the news gives him sermon ideas. His tools are positioned next to his tea mug: scissors, yellow legal pad, black felt-tip pen, and file folders. Oh, and the industrial-size bottle of Tylenol. Dad gets wicked bad headaches, migraines sometimes.

"You've been oversleeping a lot," he says.

"I've had a ton of homework." I peek under the pile of newspapers by his left elbow. Nothing. "Have you seen my keys?"

He straightens the pile. "You're graduating in two months. Why do you have so much homework?"

"Most of my teachers are insane, that's why." Keys . . . I shake the old photo bag I use for a purse. No jingling. Darn. Did I leave them in the car? I never do that.

"Kate."

Uh-oh. He's using the God Voice.

"Sit down. We need to talk."

Arguing would be a waste of time. I sigh and take my seat, keeping the table between us. "What are we talking about?"

He lines up the scissors and pens parallel to the edge of the newspaper. "College. We need to talk about college. Every time I bring it up, you change the subject."

"No, I don't. Can you write me an excuse? Homeroom is about to start."

"See? You did it again. I'm still your father, you know. Now tell me what is going on."

When Dad gets like this, all *I'm-the-father-and-I-know-best*, our tiny kitchen expands into the arctic tundra with a sink at one end, and a refrigerator and stove at the other. Wind howls across the frozen wasteland, mercury freezes.

I cross my arms over my chest. "All right, here's the deal. I'm still waiting to hear from MIT. I'm not making any decisions until I get their letter. It'll be here any day." (Totally true, every word.) "I really need that note."

He taps his lips with the end of his pen, then scribbles me an excuse. "And once you hear from MIT, we'll sit down and go over everything, all your options."

"MIT is the only option I care about." (More truth.)

"You're getting obsessed."

"A well-managed obsession can be very productive. How come you got in so late last night?"

"I got a call from a panicked mother. Her little boy was running a high fever. We took him to the ER—turned out to be an ear infection. Remember how Toby used to get those?"

I nod. "You should have heard him coughing last night. I think he should stay home from school." I pick up the excuse, fold it, and put it in my bag. "I have practice after school, and you have that chicken dinner. Don't forget. The congregation gets pissed when you don't show up."

He picks up the scissors and slices through the paper. "Don't say 'pissed.' It's crude."

"The congregation gets *perturbed* when you forget to show up at these things. Oh, and don't make any plans for me on Saturday. I'm working in the morning and getting my contacts—finally—in the afternoon."

He keeps cutting. "You're changing the subject again. I don't know why you keep avoiding this. It's not like you."

La-la-la-la-la. I am not listening. Let him have the last word. I am the child, he is the father, and all is right with the universe. I grab my books and—*ow*—that twinge again in my chest. I think I strained a pectoral muscle lifting weights for track. The books slide awkwardly against one another. My keys were sandwiched between mythology and chemistry. I toss them in the air and catch them. "When the letter comes, bring it to school, okay?"

He keeps cutting. "Have a good day. God bless, Kate."

## 2.2 | Transition Element

The church next door is dark and the stone walls give off a chill. Dad refuses to spend money on floodlights because he says churches don't need security. I shiver and hustle to my sad excuse of a motor vehicle, a Yugo named Bert.

I usually drive to school on autopilot. Not today—leaving late has landed me smack in the middle of rush-hour traffic.

This is bad. Bert fears traffic. Bert is a wuss, a tissue box on tires with a bulimic hunger for motor oil. I pet the dashboard as I turn onto the main road, and promise him a filter change if he can get me to school without overheating.

A minivan cuts in front of us and stops at the next yellow light. *Come on, lady, get the lead out.* The driver, a mom wearing big sunglasses, is either screaming or singing to the kids strapped into the back seat. Start, coast, stop. Another yellow, a long red. Shoot.

I cover the temperature gauge and jiggle my left leg. If Dad hadn't slowed me down, I'd be at school right now. *God bless.* Why does he insist on saying that? I don't inflict scientific theories on him. I don't make him contemplate the elegance of the periodic table or particle physics. He knows I'm allergic to the G-word. He does it just to annoy me.

The light turns green, and the minivan heads for the elementary school. I steer Bert to the entrance ramp of the bypass. Once we merge, I put on the hazard flashers and settle into the slow lane. The sore muscle in my chest whimpers as I wrestle the gearshift into third.

Don't get me wrong, I'm not against religion. Religion is good, apparently. Millions of people seem to enjoy it. But I'm not buying it, especially the brand-name version my dad sells. I don't see that his blessings have ever helped anything.

A line of cars passes me, horns honking, middle fingers saluting. Sometimes I wish I did have faith. If I did, I'd pray for another thousand miles on this heap. And to be accepted by MIT, of course. A full scholarship would be nice. A microwave for my dorm room, a work-study job in a decent lab. God could pay for my contacts, cure Toby's asthma, get Mitch's parents off his back about his major, and develop a cure for AIDS. If I believed in God, I'd pray all the time. Dad would croak.

We're approaching the big hill, the one that makes Bert shudder. I floor it for a second to gain some momentum, then take my foot off the gas and coast to give the engine a second to cool down before the big push.

I am not the daughter Rev. Jack Malone wants. He is not the father I need. It's as simple as that. Rev. Dad (Version 4.7) is a faulty operating system, incompatible with my software.

I downshift, accelerate, and cross my fingers. Halfway up the hill and Bert is panting, but it doesn't smell like anything is on fire. Slow and steady, eyes up.

Dad and I might be able to tolerate each other if he had a normal job. Everybody argues with their father. But nobody else has to listen to what Jesus would think about MTV, or what He would think about class rankings. Nobody else has to play the role of sweet little preacher's girl in addition to getting into college and ironing clothes and feeding the pets and making sure my brother takes his medicine.

Crap.

I should have checked Toby's peak flow reading before I left. Dad will forget. I fumble in my bag for something to write with and come up with one of Mitch's Harvard pens. I scrawl "pk flw" on the back of my left hand. We crest the hill and I pat the dashboard again. A filter change and premium gas, I swear, buddy.

### 2.2.1 ▌ Base

You're probably wondering what happened to my mom.

It was pneumonia—resistant to drugs, resistant to oxygen, hungry, fast, and fatal.

She got sick on a Thursday and died three days later. Her lungs filled up and she drowned. It took everybody by surprise. Especially the doctors.

I was in fourth grade. I didn't enter the science fair that year. Everything was blurry.

I know I am supposed to be all tragic and freaked out because my mom is dead, but sorry, I'm not. Sometimes I miss her; it's not like I'm heartless, but I've lived half of my life without her. She's like a distant aunt, someone who was fun to play with, but forgets to send birthday cards. I dream about her sometimes. I think it's about her, anyway.

### 2.3 ▌ Caustic

I park the car in the last row of the Merryweather High student lot and sprint to the door. I walk through the metal detector without setting off any alarms. I'll have to get a late pass, but that shouldn't be—

"Hold it right there, honey." The security guard stands up and walks over to me.

The guard and the metal detectors are new this year. They allow our parents to think we are safe.

The guard hitches up her pants and tries on a firm but friendly smile. "I need to see your student ID," she says.

Good God. I sigh and swing my photo bag around. The card fits in the plastic sleeve on the front flap.

She clears her throat. "Like I said, I need to see your ID."

"What?" I look at the bag. The sleeve is empty, the card gone. Oh, crap. Oh, smelly crap. "It must have fallen out in the parking lot. I had to run. Or it's in my car. I'll get it for you second period. Excuse me, I have to go. I'm way late for chem."

She slides sideways and blocks my path. "I can't let you enter the building without proper identification."

"Yes, you can. Mrs. Watson does it all the time."

"That's why Mrs. Watson was fired. I'm in charge now. I follow orders."

Deep breath. Be nice. "I'm Kate Malone. I'm ranked third in the senior class. I'm National Honor Society, a peer counselor. Look." I pull out my wallet and show her my license. "That's me."

She studies it and crosses her arms over her bosom. "There is nothing on that license that says you are a student here. You could be disgruntled. You could be hostile."

"Do I look hostile?"

"You are a teenager."

## 2.4 ▌ The Crucible

It takes ten minutes to convince Cerberus to escort me to the office, where the principal vouches for me and commends the guard for her vigilance. Good dog. By the time I make it to the science wing, room 313, first period is nearly over.

AP Chem is home: the orderly rows of lab tables, clinking glass beakers and test tubes, and the molecular models floating overhead like satellites, beaming data down to us. I'm in my element here. If I had my way, I'd study chemistry all day, with maybe a math class thrown in every once in a while for diversion.

Ms. Cummings is writing a formula on the board. She looks over her shoulder. "I was wondering if we'd see you, Kate."

I set the late pass on her desk. "Car trouble."

"I was hoping it was something more significant."

"You and me both."

Ms. Cummings moved to our district my freshman year and set up a science geek club the day she arrived. She turned me on to nanotechnology, got me over my biochem prejudice, and supervised all my science fair entries, including the one that took the national award. She is my fairy god-mother in a lab coat and goggles. I don't even hold it against her that she goes to Dad's church and sings in his choir.

Twenty-six sets of eyes follow me to my table. Twenty-six pair of lips whisper the same question. "Are you in? Are you in? Are you in? Are you in, Kate?"

I shrink smaller and smaller as I walk to the back of the room. By the time I get to my table, I have to pull myself up onto the stool looming ten feet overhead. Everybody is always into everybody else's business around here. Pisses me off.

"Well?" asks Diana Sung, my lab partner, 3.86 GPA, accepted by Rensselaer Polytechnic Institute.

"I didn't check the mail yesterday," Bad Kate lies.

"She hasn't heard yet," Diana reports to the rest of the class.

Several dweeb-kings nod smugly: Ed Davis, 3.97, accepted by every college he applied to, all fifteen of them; Omar Hakeen, 4.12 (we get extra brownie points for super-advanced honors courses), full ride to Howard University; Eric Warren, 3.84, headed to Dartmouth to study pre-med and play hockey.

I put on my safety goggles and study the boiling water bath on our hot plate. "What's their problem?"

"They have a pool going. The odds on you getting into MIT are four to one."

"For?"

Diana fiddles with the graphing calculator. "Against."

"It's just a paperwork problem. Guidance said it's happening more and more. Where's Mariah?"

"Sick. Allegedly."

Mariah Yates is waiting for her acceptance letter, too. She's wound up tighter than a psychotic terrier on crack. If she doesn't get into her top school, she'll snap. Totally. Her parents will be paying room and board at a mental hospital.

Diana uses a sharp pencil to copy the numbers from the calculator. "She's been accepted at eight other schools. There is no reason for her to freak out."

I lean closer to the boiling water in the beaker. Angry bubbles race to the top of the water and explode. Applying to only one school seemed like such a good idea at the time.

"Whatever," I say. "Let's finish this."

Our experiment is supposed to show the relationship between gas temperature and pressure. We have to stick some sealed tubes of air into beakers of cold water and hot water and figure out what the temperature does to the air pressure in the tubes. Not exactly rocket science, but fun enough. Diana has already taken the cold readings. The water in the beaker is at full boil now: bubble, bubble, toil and—

*Slam!*

Mariah Yates stands in the doorway clutching a letter to her chest, black mascara running down her face.

"I got into Stanford!" she shrieks.

Most of the class breaks into applause. A couple of guys pull out their wallets and pay up. They bet against Mariah?

Fatal error. She's just this side of crazy, yes, but it's a brilliant kind of crazy, the kind that will either go down in flames her first semester or change the world.

I write down the temperature and air pressure data and reach for the calculator. Mariah shows her letter to Ms. Cummings.

I am so very happy for her.

## 2.5 ▌ Reactants

The faded sign on the wall says the cafeteria seats five hundred. As if. At last count, the student population here at Marvelous Merryweather High was 4,317. Hence the need for "lunch" at 8:30 in the morning. Hence also the tables sized for elementary students, the theory being that if they use smaller seats, more kids will be able to squeeze in.

I head for our table and stop. It has been taken over by football players, an entire squad of shoulders and thick forearms. Not my cup of tea, football players, though a few of the lads have lovely tight ends. They smell showered, and they're eating French toast fingers. Showered men and French toast—quite an olfactory combination. My pheromones moan. Down, girl. Concentrate. Be alert. Where are my people? I squint and scan, looking for recognizable life-forms. I can't wait to get my contacts. These glasses are useless.

A red flannel figure hunkers at the far end of the table, a slumped shape I'd know anywhere.

Teri Litch.

Teri Litch reading *People* magazine, eating her federally subsidized breakfast. Every school has a Teri—the kid who peed her pants in fifth grade and sat in it all day. The kid who wore only two different outfits in seventh grade. Our Teri put on one hundred pounds in ninth grade, then stopped eating in tenth. The ugly girl, the one who smells funny, studies carpentry at vo-tech, stomps around with sawdust in her hair, and has fists like sledgehammers. Teri beat me up every year in elementary school, fall and spring. I turned the other cheek for a while, then I learned to run. Intelligent life pursues self-preservation.

Teri turns the page and glances up at me, her glasses glinting in the sun. Uh-oh, don't disturb the bear.

A purple football jersey grunts at me. "Malone."

I turn away from Teri to Brandon Figgs, my favorite tight end. We hooked up for a while last year, but I always wanted to say *shut up, can we please start kissing now because you are so dumb I want to scream.* Unfortunately, he kissed like a vacuum cleaner. It didn't last long.

"Have you seen Mitch?" I ask.

Brandon shakes his head. The player next to him says something rude. It involves Teri and his jockstrap. Do I have to give details? His buddies crack up. Brandon laughs, chokes, and dribbles milk out of his mouth, which makes everyone laugh harder. So attractive.

A flush creeps up Teri's neck.

This is where I should stick up for her. I am Kate Malone,

after all. I'm the preacher's kid, Rev. Malone's skinny little girl. I am supposed to practice all that love-your-neighbor stuff.

Teri gives me the finger.

All righty, then.

## 2.5.1 ▎Bonds

"Kate!"

The shout comes from the back of the room.

I leave Teri and the boys behind and walk to where my friends are sitting. Sunshine blazes through the glass wall that fronts an unused courtyard, backlighting them into shadow puppets. I have to shade my eyes to look at them.

"You're late, what's up?" Sara asks.

"Sunglasses, somebody, anybody? You have chosen the absolute worst table, you know."

"It feels good," Sara says with a wiggle. "Think Cancún, think Miami, think L.A."

"Think about the sun frying my eyeballs."

Sara slides her sunglasses across the table. I take off my glasses and put them on. The room mellows to a golden, SPF-protected glow.

"Thanks."

They are out of focus now, but as with Teri, I'd recognize these shapes anywhere. Sara Emery, my BF, is a self-described Wiccan Jewish poet. This would send most parents screaming to the therapist's office, but the Emerys are totally cool with it. I've been asking them to adopt me for years.

Travis Baird is to Sara as water is to fire: opposite and necessary. Trav is a freakazoid good guy with a taste for body art. The vice-principal in charge of discipline has been aching to bust him for four years. He refuses to believe that good things can come in colorful packages.

A warm hand snakes its way around my waist. My knees buckle and the hand pulls me down into the very familiar lap of Mitchell A. Pangborn III—my friend, my enemy, my lust.

"I missed you," he whispers in my ear. He kisses my neck gently and I get dizzy all over again. I look around quickly—the authorities here spaz about physical displays of affection, even if you get good grades. No adults in sight. I toss Sara's sunglasses on the table, tilt my head, and kiss him good morning. He shifts a little in his seat. His lap is very happy to see me.

Mitch and I started fighting in sixth grade. It was a Clash of the Titans for years: Scientific Genius (me) vs. Humanities Nerd (him). Weapons: report cards, GPAs, SATs, and AP scores. For a while we used to arm wrestle, too, but that stopped after eighth grade because he grew five inches and gained an unfair amount of leverage.

Last September we made a bet. Whoever got accepted into their top school early decision could make the other person do whatever he or she wanted. Anything. No limits. Harvard welcomed Mitch with open arms. MIT deferred me.

I thought for sure he'd make me do something humiliating in front of the entire student body. Instead, he took me out to dinner. I still don't know which was more shocking: the fact that I got deferred, or that Mitchell "Obnoxious" Pangborn was a flame-throwing, heart-quivering, jeans-creaming, phenomenal kisser. It was a good date. It was a very good date.

So after six years of hating him, why did I start liking him? He's smart. He gets my jokes. He has black hair and gray eyes that remind me of the ocean after a storm. And he has freckles, though I haven't told him I think they're cute. He understands about my dad and all the crap at my house. He even congratulated me when I wound up with a higher class rank. And like I said, the boy knows how to kiss.

And kiss . . .

And kisssss . . .

The kisses are necessary. When we're kissing, we can't argue. He still thinks that science is the root of all evil. I think that going to an Ivy League college to study history is sort of like winning the lottery and giving away all the money. What's the point? His parents agree with me. They want him to be practical, to study something that has a career attached to it. But they've been getting kind of harsh, so I've decided to argue less and kiss more.

"Should I get you kids a hotel room?" Sara asks.

I pull back, then grip Mitch's shoulders as another wave of dizziness crashes over me.

He studies my face and frowns. "You have raccoon eyes. What time did you get to bed last night?"

"I don't know. I didn't look at the clock." I move off his lap and onto the seat next to him and put the sunglasses back on. Sara pushes a steaming cup of coffee to me and slides over the little cardboard box of coffee fixings.

"You do look wicked tired," she says. "You're going to get sick if you keep this up."

I tear open two blue packets, pour them in the cup, add dairy creamer, and stir with a thin wooden stick. I blow ripples across the surface of the coffee and sip. Aaahhh; aspartame, gelatin, caffeine, and hot, melted Styrofoam.

"I'm fine," I say. "It's not a big deal."

Mitch snaps his coffee stirrer in half. "You went running last night, didn't you? Late."

Falling in love makes you stupid. You say things that you should probably keep to yourself. A couple of weeks ago, Mitch thought that running at night was cool.

He points the broken end of the stick at me. "It's not good, Malone. It's not safe."

"It's perfectly safe. You worry too much, Pangborn."

Mitch breaks the coffee stirrer again. I reach across him for the doughnut bag and my pec twangs again. Damn, that hurts. There are two doughnuts left—plain and glazed. Glazed is an indulgent doughnut, breakfast for spoiled rah-rahs. I take the plain.

Sara cuddles up to Travis and kisses his skull. "Wake up, stud boy."

Travis has been snoring quietly, his shaved head reflecting the sun. He pulls the overnight shift at Superfresh a couple of times a month. It's good for his bank account, but makes staying awake in school next to impossible.

Sara sets a coffee cup in front of his nose. His nostrils twitch, then he groans and sits up. After a gulp of coffee, he blinks and focuses on Sara's face, Sara's lips. He groans again. This boy has it so bad for her, it's a thing of beauty. They've been going strong for four years. This worries me. What are they going to do in September? It's not like Trav can move into her dorm room (though I probably shouldn't give him the idea). Shouldn't they be cutting their losses, closing doors, getting ready to pack it up and say good-bye?

They don't care. They R IN LUV.

Sarah scrapes chocolate frosting off her doughnut and applies it to Travis's lips. Then she sucks it off.

"Do you have to do that in public?" Mitch asks.

Sara unsticks herself from Travis's face. "Yes," she purrs, before going back to work.

Mitch steals Travis's coffee stirrer and breaks it in half. I keep my eyes on my cup. "Mariah got into Stanford," I say.

"She'll burn out."

"Yeah."

He slips his arm around my waist again and squeezes once. "Don't worry. You're in. The letter is on its way. And if they screwed up and didn't admit you, you'll just go some-place else and transfer. Chill, Kate. It's going to be okay."

I dunk my doughnut in my coffee. They're letting me in. They will. The end of my doughnut crumbles and sinks to the bottom of the cup. They have to.

At the front of the cafeteria, the football players explode in laughter. The red-checked flannel Teri Litch shape rises and walks to a different table. She sits. The team rises and follows her. It's a game. Tease Teri.

The team chants quietly.

"Bitch. Bitch. Bitch."

The good news is that they aren't harassing me or my friends. The bad news is that they are harassing Teri. The hair on the back of my neck stands up. We are looking at a situation here.

The noise causes Sara and Travis to come up for air.

"I don't know what kind of bug is up their collective butt . . ." Sara says.

Travis mumbles something.

". . . but they've been dogging Teri all period. Three times she's changed tables and they keep following."

"So you're going to run to her rescue?" I ask.

"Please. Do I look mental?" Sara sputters. "But still."

"They'll get bored," Travis predicts. "Picking on Tubby Teri is a middle school game."

"She's not tubby anymore," I point out. "She's all muscle. They should be recruiting her for the defensive line."

The team chants quietly so as not to alert the cafeteria monitors gossiping in the kitchen. "Bitch. Bitch. Bitch."

Teri has had enough. I tense, waiting for her to throw one of the morons into a trash can. I hate days that start with cafeteria fights. But wait. . . . Teri is walking away. She pauses only to drop her orange juice carton in the garbage.

"Wow!" Travis exclaims. "Excellent pacifist response."

"I bet she's going to burn down the locker room," Sara says. "Remember what she did to Amber?"

Amber, a cheerleader, made the mistake of telling Teri she should bathe more often. They never proved who put the dead skunk in Amber's pearl-white Jetta, but it didn't matter. The message was scent.

The clock is ticking down. We only have two minutes left. Mitch collects our trash and Sara puts the unused creamers in her purse. The cafeteria ladies cackle in the distance. I give the sunglasses back to Sara and put on my own nasty specs. Yuck—the world returns in cold, horrid focus.

"She's ba-ack," Sara says, nodding her head toward Teri Litch, who is storming across the front of the room. "Forgot her books."

The second hand sweeps past the numbers on the face of the clock, rushing to the bell. The football team rises. Teri Litch walks over to them. It happens in slow motion, a ballet. *Pas de duel.* Teri lifts a thick history book and swings it in a wide arc until it smashes into the mouth of Art Smith, defensive tackle. Art flies backward. A tooth sails over the team and lands near the door.

One freeze frame.

"Fight!" bellows a bull.

Action.

The team goes nuts. Teri plows her meaty fist into the side of Brandon Figgs's head and he goes down without a word. Then Teri goes down, not even her red shirt visible under the shouts and the arms and the legs of angry boys.

We have to do something. We can't walk away from a traffic accident in the middle of the cafeteria. Sara gets there first, screaming like a banshee, her black hair a flag waving behind her. It's hard to tell who is fighting whom. The team is shoving, punching, pulling—each other. Sara wades in, plucking at sleeves with her long, pinchy fingers. Other people flow into the room, some fighting, some not-so-fighting.

A girl wails in the corner. "You guuuys, cut it out! You guuuys, cut it out!"

This is the suburbs. With the exception of Teri Litch, nobody knows how to land a real punch. A thought flashes by in record time, and I can't keep it from unfolding—these guys are lucky she didn't bring her daddy's shotgun to school.

Travis yanks on football jerseys, pulling the scrum apart one body at a time. I should do something, I know I should.

The wailing continues, pitching up to a whine. "Cut it out, guuuuys! Guuuys, cut it out!"

Teri Litch's glasses skitter across the floor.

Mitch, oh God, Mitchell Pangborn. He climbs up on the table next to the fray and raises his arms over his head to form a giant O. He looks like an apprentice mime.

"What the hell are you doing?" I shout.

"Making a statement," he answers. "Zero tolerance." He shakes his arms once for emphasis. "Get it? Zero?"

Sometimes it's hard to believe he got into Harvard.

"Get down from there, Pangborn," I say. "This is no time for performance art."

The security squad finally arrives, followed by the principal and all sorts of pink-faced adults. Teri rises up from the pack, cursing at the top of her lungs. They grab her arms. Her watch is ripped off and falls to the floor.

The bell rings. It's over. The fight is over. Sara flicks her hair out of her face and stalks past me muttering. "Oppressive bastards, think they own the place. I told them that karma's going kick their asses. . . . "

Security hustles Teri out of the room. She's screaming that they broke her watch, that somebody better buy her a new one. The football players fade into the crowd, except for Art, the guy who lost the tooth. He wants to file a complaint.

I pick up Teri's glasses. The nosepiece is grimy and the lenses are scratched. I fold the arms and set them on top of her books. Her watch has disappeared.

Mitch hops off the table, stumbling a bit when he hits the floor. I look over at him and say, "This day has been really—"

He grabs my face and kisses me. He tastes like coffee and doughnuts and toothpaste. I kiss him back until I have to breathe.

"Thanks," I say. "I needed that."

## 2.6 | Boron

Third period English. Hell. Smell the sulfur, feel the flames. English is worse than a waste of time—it robs valuable brain cells that could be doing something practical.

I sit by the window. Mitchell slips into the seat in front of me.

"Get out your texts?" Miss Devlin whispers.

I am here under protest. I was promised that Mythology 231 would be a multiple-choice English class, with little "discussion" and no essays. I hate essays.

"Please get out your texts, your notebooks, and some-thing to write with? With which to write? You know what I mean." Miss Devlin is a student teacher, exactly three years older than I am. She has nothing to teach me, null, nada, nut'in. A teacher (a good teacher) is composed of molecules of education and intelligence, bonded together by patience and passion. Miss Devlin breaks down into equal parts des-peration, hair spray, and mints. Her bonds are not strong. She could fly apart at any minute.

"Much better," Miss Devlin says. "Now who wants to tell us the story of the birth of Athena?" She waddles down the aisle checking for contraband headphones and comic books. I bet her panty hose are slipping off her butt. "Athena? Daughter of Zeus? It was in last night's reading?"

Mitch raises his hand. Of course he did the reading. He probably read it in the original Greek.

I study the parking lot. Time in English class passes so slowly, I swear I can see the cars rusting. After about a mil-lion years, a dented gray van pulls in and cruises the aisles looking for an open space. I sure hope they brought their IDs.

I blink. No way. It can't be. It's the Godmobile, my father's church van. And it's looking for a place to park. I lean forward, forgetting about Athena and Zeus and Mitchell, who can be absurd, but tastes good. The van hesitates in front of an open spot marked for disabled parking, then moves on. I sit back in my seat, flash-frozen. Why is Dad here? He hates coming here. We fight about it. He says it's unnecessary because I "have everything under control" and other assorted garbage which really means I am on my own.

Another layer of ice forms. Maybe someone is dead. Maybe it's Toby, who is a perverted moron, but he's my brother, and what if a bee stung him and he had a bad allergic reaction and his throat swelled closed and he choked to death in math class? He hates math. What a horrible way to die.

Stop. Breathe.

No one is dead, no one is dying. Get a grip, think happy thoughts. Dad has the letter. The Fat Letter. The fat letter from the thank-you-Jesus Massachusetts Institute of Technology and Salvation. Holy Mother, I'm going to Cambridge. I don't need a safety school or a backup plan because everything is working out just the way I planned it. The ice shell around me melts, the sun comes out, and a rainbow streaks across the sky. The letter has details from Student Housing and Financial Aid and a note from the track coach welcoming me aboard and my summer reading list and advice to incoming freshmen (that's me!). My temperature soars past 98.6 degrees Fahrenheit. I am burning with joy one-oh-one, one-oh-two, one-oh-three. I fry this high school skin to a crisp and emerge from the ashes, a college student. Get me out of here, I'm free, I am so gone. What is the point of sitting here? Why waste Miss Devlin's valuable time?

The Godmobile stops and parks in a visitor's slot, next to the nurse's car. I'm halfway out of my seat before I realize it.

"Kate Malone? Is something wrong?" Miss Devlin asks.

Delete that thought. Reality intrudes. The mail never, ever, ever comes earlier than four o'clock. There is no way on earth he can have that letter. No way. I sit back down. "Leg cramp," I say. "My gluteus maximus hurts."

Mitch chokes back a laugh. Miss Devlin knows nothing about my anatomy, but he does.

The door of the Godmobile opens. It can't be the letter. It can't be the letter. Dad sits there for a second, then he takes off his seat belt and gets out of the van. I hope it's the letter. He looks very small from up here.

Miss Devlin draws a family tree of the Greek gods on the board. Athena was born from the skull of Zeus, jumped out as a full-sized adult, dressed for battle. (Bad Kate screams: Why do we need to know this?) Time drips off the clock while I keep one eye on the door and the other on the parking lot. This is the type of torture that Zeus would approve of.

Dad returns to the Godmobile just before the period ends. He's wearing the Serious Loving Pastor Face. Dad is on duty. It was a false alarm. I have to breathe again. Damn.

Miss Devlin writes out our homework on the board: *Study the incarnations of Athena. Greek vocab definitions (2 pts ea.!): academy, hubris, catalyst, catharsis, agape. Essay on Artemis due next week!*

I flip open my agenda book, every hour penned in, every

minute accounted for. At the top of the page, in the right-hand corner, in red ink, is a fat number one. One more day. I started counting ninety-three days ago, when my application was shunted from the Early Decision to the Everyone Else pile. It feels like a lot longer than that. But now we're down to real time, meat time, flesh and gristle time. One . . . more . . . day . . . until the waiting is over. The letter will come and everything will be okay.

Bad Kate wants to stand on the desk, rip off her shirt, and dance like a wild woman. Good Kate won't allow that. She draws a heart around the red number one.


## 2.7 ▌ Solubility

The Springville coach calls us to the starting line. "Hurry up, men. Ladies, too. Let's get this over with."

"Move it, you slackers," Coach Reid shouts.

This is not officially a meet. Coach Reid and the Springville coach cooked up an unofficial "scrimmage," a 5K race between the long-distance runners of the two teams. The spring track season depresses cross-country runners, because we can only officially compete in the two-mile runs. We like to go the distance.

Cross-country was made for me. I'm small and wiry and tenacious as hell. Any fool can run fast on an expensive track with lane markers, starting blocks, and a tailwind. Show me a girl who can slog it out against driving sleet, wearing mud-caked shoes and a wool cap that drips down the back of her neck—now that's a runner.

The windchill is below forty: spring in Syracuse. At least it's not snowing. I pull my orange cap down so that it covers my ears and smack my orange-mittened hands together to keep the blood flowing. All this orange against my purple Merryweather uniform makes me look like a psychedelic Teletubby.

Focus on the race, Malone. Focus on the race. Win. My glasses slide down my nose. I push them back up with my mitten.

"Take your marks." The Springville coach lifts his arm in the air, pretending he's holding a starting gun. "Bam!" He shoots the air.

I hesitate, freeze on the line. My glasses slip again. The screws must be loose, but I can't worry about that now. I take them off, toss them at the coach, and run.

I jog at seventy percent to let my legs warm up. Let the hotshot underclassmen dash ahead. No one sprints for 3.1 miles. I'll catch them in the end. I pick up the pace half a mile in, when my gears are oiled. Sweat beads between my shoulder blades, under my breasts, at my waistband. My left Achilles tendon aches. I run faster. The sweat blooms into the rain that soaks my uniform. I pass one body, two, three. Keep your eyes on the ground, Kate, don't turn an ankle. Slow down to skitter over sodden leaves, accelerate uphill, pass a pack of six. The Achilles relaxes and stretches, my thighs heat up.

I shift gears again. Eighty percent. My dad used to run long distance. He still wears his marathon T-shirts sometimes. You'll never catch me doing a marathon. I love to run, but come on, twenty-six miles? That's wack. Mom was a sprinter. She could do the hundred-yard dash in just a few heartbeats.

The path wanders through a dark pine grove. The air is colder here. Focus, Malone. Run faster. My feet feel out the path, testing the traction of the wet needles. Set the pace, find the rhythm, find the pattern. The run-till-you-win pattern: stepstepstepstep—breathe . . . breathe . . . stepstepstepstep—breathe . . . breathe . . . One more sound, my braid smacking against my spine like a rope against a flagpole. Stepstepstepstep. *Thwackthwackthwackthwack.* Breathe . . . breathe . . . Running is the mathematical sport. My races are a consistently balanced equation: effort=result.

Relax, Malone. Relax. Run faster.

The day jumps back at me in jagged fragments. The Godmobile in the wrong place, my father wearing the wrong face. Stepstepstepstep. *Thwackthwackthwackthwack.* Dad never comes to school, not even for track meets. Did somebody get busted? Try to kill themselves? Was he called in to counsel Teri? (He'll have a black eye tonight if he did.) He just looked so weird, so small and not Dadlike.

Lactic acid is weighing down my legs. I haven't passed anyone in a while. Am I in front of the pack? My Achilles hurts again, and that stupid, pulled pec. Breathe . . . breathe. Control the mind. Need a positive, rhythmic phrase. Almost there . . . al-most there. Oh, so close . . . oh, so close.

Another phrase wells up from the mud on the bottom of my sneakers: no envelope—no envelope—no envelope. Bad rhythm, out of sync. I stumble and have to slow down for a second. Negative thoughts are not allowed. Run faster.

New phrase: MIT! MIT! MIT! MIT! Much better.

Stepstepstepstep . . . *Thwackthwackthwackthwack* . . . won't let you in . . . won't let you in . . . won't let you in.

Another tight turn, no other runners. Did they all go the wrong way? I check my watch, bring it up to my face so I can see the numbers. I should be near the school by now. I'm on pace to be crossing the finish line.

My feet slow down, then stop.  The rain changes to hail.


I went in exactly the wrong direction in the woods. I am dead last, so last they aren't even timing me. The Springville coach, wearing a winter parka now, approaches me. "You must be Katie Malone. I think these are yours." He hands me my glasses.

"Kate," I correct automatically.

"Rhymes with late," he says with a chuckle.

"Ha-ha," I say. Steam rises from my head when I take off my cap. I wring the water out of it and stick it back on, then I put on my glasses. The coach's face is fluid and wavy.

He grins. "Got lost, huh? Bet it was in the woods." He is oddly cheerful about this. I bet he's wearing thermal underwear.

The Merryweather bus pulls up alongside us. I yank my cap down over my face and feel my way up the steps.

## 2.8 ▌ Reduction

When we get back to school, I beeline from the bus to my car. I take Mitch's crimson Harvard sweatshirt out of the trunk and put it on, then take a water jug and refill the radiator. My nose hairs are frozen. I am soaked to my underwear. I want to stand in a hot shower until the marrow in my bones boils.

Bert's engine starts right away and he steers us toward home. I got lost on the course. How stupid. How stupid, pathetic, lame, ridiculous, moronic, and, and . . . I need another adjective. I'm sure there's a better word for this feeling. It's like pouring vinegar into baking soda and having it vomit all over the lab table while a panel of distinguished judges observes.

I flick on the turn signal, check my mirror, check the mirror again—God, I look like a refugee—and merge onto the highway. I hate merging. I can never tell if I'm supposed to speed up or slow down. Just a few more hours, Malone. MIT. MIT. The letter is coming. Hang in there.

The traffic thins as I approach my exit. My teeth chatter. Is it possible to knock out a filling by chattering too hard? I'm going to stand in the shower, then drink hot chocolate and curl into my bed with all the extra blankets and a heating pad and Mr. Spock, and even Sophia can join us if she'll contribute body heat.

Off the exit, skim down a few country roads, past a dead strip mall, past a newly plowed field. Past the blinking yellow, turn right. I can see the church steeple and the roof of our house. Quarter of a mile later, here's the church, here's the steeple, open the doors, and see all the . . . dear God.

I pull in the driveway. The parking lot is overflowing with cars.

It's Chicken and Biscuit Wednesday.

"Oh, Katie, thank heavens you're here," Betty clucks as she rummages through our silverware drawer. "We can't find the big box of spoons. You know the one."

Betty is our church secretary, organist, and official busy-body. She is six inches shorter than me, three times as wide, and smells of face powder. Each Christmas she knits me a tacky cardigan that I pretend to hate but secretly adore. I am going to put one on as soon as I get out of the shower.

She closes the first drawer and opens another. "I checked everywhere in the church. They have to be here."

"I hav-v-v-ven't seen them."

My capillaries are jammed with ice floes. I grab my brother's jacket off the back of a kitchen chair and slip it on.

Betty stares at the water running down my legs.

I rummage through the pile of newspapers on the table. "Where's Toby?"

"He's playing video games in the family room. That cough of his sounds better."

"Good." I lift up the pile and look under it. "Where's the mail?"

"What mail?"

"Our mail. The family mail. My mail."

"Well, it's not on that table."

I inhale slowly, counting to ten. "I know. I just looked."

"A boy called for you, that cute one, with the freckles."

"Mitchell."

"I think you should marry him, Katie. Jesus would approve."

(Jesus lives in the back of Betty's television set. They chat. A lot.)

"I'm not getting married until after graduate school, Betty. I just want the mail. Where's Dad?"

Betty's left eye twitches. "I don't know. Are you sure you don't know where those spoons are?"

I count to sixty-four in base two. "Betty, when you see Dad, tell him I desperately need the mail. I'll be in the shower, thawing."

Betty rifles through our junk drawer. "Oh, no, dear, you don't want to shower now. The hot water's all gone."

"Gone? But . . . " I shiver at the horrifying vision of showering at school, or worse, at Betty's house.

"Your boiler is broken. You don't have any hot water." She pulls out an ancient silver tablespoon. The spoon part is bent up and back, making it look like a golf club. Betty slips it into her pocket. "No telling when it'll be fixed. You might as well come over to church and help." She closes the drawer with a dramatic sigh. "Of course, if you want to stay here, well, I won't tell you what to do. Even if the Catholics are coming."

The word "Catholics" is whispered, as in *those people*. Betty is five hundred years old, old enough to remember the Catholics and Protestants at war.

"The Catholics won't bite, Betty, I promise. They're nice, normal people, just like me and . . . just like lots of folks. And I'd love to help, but like I said, I've had a long day, a long, bad day. You'll have to do chicken and biscuits without me tonight."

Heavy footsteps announce the approach of the Presence. Betty looks over my shoulder and smiles.

"Good evening, Reverend," she says. "My, don't you look handsome!"

## 2.9 ▍ Surface Tension

The church kitchen is crammed with ladies hovering over giant vats of bubbling food. It's hot in here, and it smells like a chicken sauna. When I walk in, the ladies smile at me, then point to the sink. They're a bit phobic about handwashing. I set my watch in a chipped teacup on a shelf above the sink and scrub my hands. The water is hot enough to melt wax. If our boiler doesn't get fixed, I could always bathe in this sink.

The ladies have prepared the dinner with military precision. The food has been purchased, chopped up, and cooked. They always know how much to make, even though they never know how many people are coming. (This may fall under the heading of a religious miracle.) The dozen cardboard boxes on the far counter will be filled with meals for the poor and elderly. Put these ladies in charge of the United Nations and we'd have an end to world hunger in a month.

Ms. Cummings rushes in carrying two heavy grocery bags. "Sorry I'm late. I couldn't find lemonade anywhere," she tells the ladies. "Kate! Did it come?"

I scrub under my nails. "Nope."

She puts the bags on the counter. "I can't believe it's taking so long. Is there anything I can do? Do you need to talk or something?"

I dry my hands on a blue-striped towel and pick up a ladle. "No, thanks. I'm all good." Before she can say anything else, I scoot over to the food line.

Chicken and Biscuit Night is simple and profitable. Pay your money and you get a plate and utensils wrapped in a paper napkin. You can choose one biscuit or two. Hand me your plate and I ladle on pieces of chicken and gravy as fast as I can, trying to remember to smile. Drinks are at the end of the line. Desserts are on the preschool table by the upright piano.

The line moves. Dip, ladle, don't drip. Smile, nod—next! Dip, ladle, don't drip. Smile, nod—next! The Kate-a-tron has been activated. Dip, ladle, don't drip. Smile, nod—next!

"Howdy, Miss Kate. How's it going?" An old man hands me his plate. Mr. Lockheart, our handyman, my savior. One of Dad's strays. Some of the kitchen ladies don't like the fact that he drinks whiskey, but I don't see any of them offering to patch the roof or clean out the nest of squirrels in the attic.

I pile three biscuits on his plate. "Mr. Lockheart, I am so happy to see you." I dig deep in the pot for hunks of chicken. "Our boiler is broken and we don't have any hot water."

He nods once. "Yeah, I heard." He rubs the white stubble on his neck. "Coulda lost the pilot light. That'd be bad, gas in the basement."

The fellow behind him, a farmer, leans in. "Gas would mean an explosion."

"That'd be bad, too," says Mr. Lockheart. He stares at his plate. I pour on the gravy slowly.

"Course, it could be a loose wire, electric problem," the farmer says.

"Or the ignition switch," muses Mr. Lockheart. "That goes at the wrong time, and boom, you got another explosion."

An executive-type dad fidgets behind the farmer. He butts in. "Can you discuss explosions at your table, please? Some of us have things to do tonight."

Mr. Lockheart ignores him. "Could be the darned thing just died. It's old. I'll take a look after I eat some."

"Great," I say, handing back his plate. "Could you try to fix it tonight?"

"I'll do my best, Miss Kate," he says solemnly. "Hey, the reverend told me you was running in a big race today. You beat 'em?"

His watery eyes open wide, his smile shows brown,

chipped teeth. His wife and children were killed years ago when he drove the family car into a snowplow on Route 81 during a blizzard. He didn't drink much before then.

"Yes, Mr. Lockheart. I beat 'em. I beat all of them by a mile."

"That's my girl!" he cackles. He leans over and gives me a smelly kiss on the middle of my forehead.

"Thanks, Mr. Lockheart. Don't forget the boiler."

The farmer gets two biscuits. The ExecuDad gets one, and I'll be darned, but I can only find flakes of chicken for him. Shucks.

The line shuffles forward and I keep ladling. I'm warmer now, and I don't think my own particular body odor is stronger than anyone else's in here, or maybe it's the smell of the cooked chicken that masks everything. The tables have filled up, and I think the (whisper) *Catholics* are mingling. Chicken and Biscuit Night makes more sense to me than Sunday morning services. If my father ever decides to talk to me about religion again, I'll point that out to him. People who avoid his sermons turn up here every month.

"Kate?"

It's Sara. "I've been calling and e-mailing constantly. You've been, like, nowhere." She points at me. "What happened? You look terrible."

The man behind Sara interrupts. "Excuse me, but some of us are hungry."

Another ExecuDad. What is it with these guys? I dump some gravy on his biscuits, then Ms. Cummings appears next to me and takes my ladle. "Go ahead and eat, Kate. You must be starving."

I take three biscuits (my wages) and an extra-large helping of chicken and gravy and scoot out of the ladle line. Sara and I take a table in the corner.

Sara strikes people as a vegetarian, save-the-whales type chick, but she loves eating meat. She just says little prayers to whatever she's eating, thanking it for the sacrifice. She chews her first bite of chicken in silence.

Prayer's over. She swallows.

"So why are you here?" I ask.

"Well, Mitch was IMing Travis and Travis was talking to me so I heard how you almost had a heart attack in English because you thought your dad had the letter and then I got a message from Amy and she said you blew out your knee at the track meet but she always exaggerates but since I hadn't heard from you I figured I should come over." She pauses to inhale. "I thought you could use some moral support."

I plop one of my gravy-soaked biscuits on her plate. "You are the best friend in the universe. In this entire plane of reality."

"*Et toi aussi, ma chérie.* Now tell me."

I fill her in on everything that sucked about the day while we eat. The noise is at peak pitch now, the har-har-hars and ho-ho-hos of good jokes told on a full stomach. The kitchen ladies come out to watch the crowd with satisfied looks on their faces. My brother is laughing with his friends and he hasn't coughed once. Dad is working the room like a pro, stopping at each table for a joke or two, pats on the back, a few heartfelt glances. Ms. Cummings brings him a plate of food. He takes a seat between the Catholic priest and a woman in a purple sweater who can't stop blushing.

My dad's a real charmer. It's not that he's hot—just the opposite: he's shortish, with gray hair and wrinkles. But he must beam security rays. Or maybe women get off on the man-of-God thing. There is always a divorcée or widow trying to get her claws into him. Not that they have a chance. When I was a kid, I overheard him tell somebody that he buried his heart when he buried Mom. It took me a long time to figure out what that meant.

"Is that Jell-O over there?" Sara asks.

I blink back into real time. "It's alive," I warn her. "You should not eat food that moves."

She pushes away from the table and tucks her hair behind her ears. "I want three helpings."

I tag along behind her as she walks to the dessert table. "I'm serious, Sara."

She giggles. "Jell-O is the secret to good mental health. Oooh, look, this one has nuts."

I shiver. Nuts do not belong in Jell-O. I take a slice of apple pie.

On the way back to our table, I catch a glimpse of red. Someone wearing a red flannel shirt is standing in the kitchen with her back toward us.

"Sara," I hiss. "Is that Teri Litch?"

Sara looks. "Can't be. Amy said she got arrested. The guy whose tooth she knocked out? His parents are pressing charges. Are you sure you don't want any of this?"

"I'll be right back."

The kitchen ladies have shifted into cleanup mode. Betty stands on a step stool in front of the sink, her arms in soapy water up to her elbows. Other ladies are attacking the counters with Comet and the cutting boards with bleach. The floor has been swept and the trash removed. The boxes for shut-ins and the poor are packed and gone. There is no sign of Teri.

I was seeing things. I've got Teri Litch on the brain, post-traumatic stress from watching the fight in the cafeteria. I really need some sleep. I reach around Betty and take the chipped teacup off the shelf.

It's empty. My watch is gone.

"Was Teri here?" I ask Betty.

She stops scrubbing. "That big Litch girl?"

"The one and only. Was she here?"

"She's gone, honey," says a woman drying a pot.

"She took my watch."

"Oh, no," Betty says. "She couldn't do a thing like that. She was sweet as can be."

Betty sends Christmas cards to mass murderers on death row.

A couple of the other ladies have slowed the pace of their scrubbing. They know Litch family stories that go back generations. The oldest woman peels off her yellow rubber gloves with a snap.

"She just left, Kate. If you hurry, you might catch her."

## 2.10 ▌ Elastic Collision

I spot Teri Litch's back crossing the graveyard. I want my watch back.

Kate = bull on a rampage. Teri = red flag.

I wait until she's moving down the hill before I jog after her. Here's my plan:

1. Make sure that she really has it.

2. Ask her for it. Nicely.

3. Ask her again. Firmly.

4. Walk away humiliated when she laughs.

I need a new plan.

I skirt the cemetery fence and stay low. I don't want her to see me yet, and she might look back, though it's unlikely, because if there was ever anybody born without a guilty conscience, it's Formerly Tubby Teri Litch. I stick to the shadows. This is kind of fun. Maybe I could be a combination Nobel–prizewinning chemist and international spy.

Plan #2

1. Make sure she has watch.

2. Tackle her.

3. Take watch by force.

4. Run like hell.

That one might work. Statistically speaking, the proba-
bility is not out of range.

"What about the consequences?" I hear the voice of
Mitchell "Afraid of His Own Shadow" Pangborn as clearly as
if he were standing next to me. I look around. No Mitch. He's
not here. It's just me and the dead people and Teri pulling
out of sight at the bottom of the hill. I am hallucinating my
boyfriend's voice, another sign that I need more sleep.
Consequences. Mitchell is very big on consequences, which
explains his virginity. Mine, too, for that matter.

Screw it. I want my watch back. It used to be my mom's.

I trot down the hill and crouch by the crumbling stone
fence. Teri walks past the old barn. Her fists are in her pocket and her sleeves are pulled all the way down, covering her
wrists. But I know she's got it.

As she heads toward the house, I tiptoe into the shadows
of the barn and crouch behind the pickup truck. This barn is
just about dead. The next good storm will flatten it. The
Litches sold off the last of their cows after Mr. Litch went to
jail. If they had any sense, they'd sell the land, too, and get
out of here.

Teri pauses on the porch steps to watch a red Toyota
hatchback come up the driveway. A witness; this could be
helpful. The driver gets out. It's Ms. Cummings. Excellent—
a reliable witness who will take my side no matter what.

Teri lights a cigarette while Ms. Cummings takes something out of the back seat. The smoke filters up to the dim porch light. Ms. Cummings carries a box, a shut-in chicken-and-biscuit dinner box, to the porch and speaks quietly.

Teri reaches for the doorknob. A-ha! Step one accomplished. My watch is on her wrist. I can't believe her. Not only did she flat out steal it—from a church basement, I'd like to point out—she has the balls to wear it. I grind my feet in the dirt, unsure of what to do. Step two, "tackle her," seems highly theoretical right now.

Teri turns toward where I'm hiding and squints through her glasses. Her left eye is bruised and swollen from the cafeteria fight. She points to me.

Damn.

"Hey, Kate!" Teri calls loudly. "You coming in?"

Ms. Cummings is startled. She looks toward the shadows. "Kate?"

Double damn. How am I going to explain this? I just wanted my watch back, then a long hot shower, a bag of Chee·tos, maybe a couple of hours on-line.

"Come on in, Katie." Teri sounds like a carnival barker. "Meet the family."


## 2.11 ▌ Half-Life

In the middle of the Litch living room there are two kitchen chairs, a couch, and a television tuned to a game show, full volume. Broken furniture is piled against the walls, along with file cabinets, a lawn tractor, and a folded-up playpen. A wicker basket of plastic fruit rests on the tractor seat—red apples, two pears, and an orange, all of them covered in crayon graffiti. The ceiling is stained brown from cigarette smoke. The arrangement is lighted by two floor lamps plugged into extension wires that snake under the couch.

"It's a very old house," says Ms. Cummings. "The original section must pre-date the Civil War."

"I bet."

Just beyond the reach of the light I can see a small rocking chair in the corner. In fact, the whole corner looks like it was set up for a little kid. The floor is covered with a brightly colored *Sesame Street* rug that is scattered with plastic blocks and metal cars. More cars and trucks are jumbled in an old Easter basket. The bookcase under the window is loaded with books and puzzles. The corner is not tidy, but it is clean.

Ms. Cummings shifts the box to her hip. "I didn't know you were friends with Teri."

"I'm not. She stole something from me."

Before she can answer, Teri guides a tiny woman into the room. The woman inches across the floorboards in scuffed slippers. She's not wearing glasses, but it's clear she can't see well. She keeps one hand floating lightly in the air in front of her.

Teri leads the woman to the couch. She sits, barely making a dent on the cushion. Two bobby pins keep her blonde hair out of her face. Her nose is flat and crooked, her eyes vague, her mouth thin. A pink scar interrupts her left eyebrow. It makes her look permanently confused. Even with the nice hair, this is the kind of woman you look at and think "bag lady."

"This is my mom," Teri says.

I look to my teacher for a clue.

"It's good to see you again, Mrs. Litch," Ms. Cummings says. She sets the box on the floor, steps forward, and gently squeezes one of Mrs. Litch's hands. "I'm Amanda Cummings, from the church. We met a few weeks ago."

Mrs. Litch's face relaxes. "Yes. Thank you for coming." Her voice is too young for her face. "Have a seat, please."

"No, I can't. I just dropped a few things off for dinner."

"For just a minute?"

Ms. Cummings sits on a kitchen chair. "Okay, but I don't want to intrude."

Teri sits on the other chair. "Why don't you sit down, Kate? Sit next to Mom."

Why don't I run out the door screaming? I want my watch back, that's why. It's worth more than my car. She'd better not be stretching the band. It looks tight on her.

I sit on the couch. Mrs. Litch turns her face to me and extends her hand. I was waiting for a whiff of beer or whiskey, but she smells a little like lemon. I, on the other hand, reek of sweat and stewed chicken.

"I'm Kate," I say, shaking the cool hand. "Kate Malone."

"Kate is Rev. Malone's daughter. She goes to school with Theresa," Ms. Cummings explains.

"How nice," says Mrs. Litch.

"Oh, it's great," Teri says.

"That's a cool watch you're wearing, Theresa," I say.

The scar over Mrs. Litch's eye twitches just a hair. Someone loses a thousand dollars on the game show and the audience groans.

"It looks just like my watch. In fact, I can't find mine. Have you seen it?"

Teri takes a deep breath. I shrink down to a size one. She can't beat me up, not in front of her mother and a teacher.

Can she?

I am saved from certain death by the arrival of a small, blond boy. Or rather, a NASCAR race car disguised as a small, blond boy. He motors into the room, a red metal Corvette in his left hand, a small ambulance missing its wheels in his right. His eyes are the color of a clean spring sky. He's wearing jeans, red sneakers, and a faded pajama top. As he runs around the room, he makes engine noises, shifting gears up and down, squealing tires. A diaper rustles under his pants.

"Come here, boy," says Mrs. Litch.

The little guy climbs into her lap and hides his face against her shoulder. He peeks at me once. You could get lost in those eyes; they're heartbreakers.

"That's Mikey," Teri says. "He's two."

Mikey peeks at me again and smiles. He has dimples and

tiny Tic Tac teeth. I put my hand out. Mikey grabs my finger for a second, then lets go and hides his face again. Another contestant is trying for big money on the television. Teri turns up the sound of the audience roaring. She'll pound the snot out of me later, I guess.

"I really should be going," Ms. Cummings says as she stands.

"So soon?" asks Mrs. Litch.

Teri stares at the television, her arms crossed over her chest. The wrist with the stolen watch is hidden. I push myself off the couch.

"Me, too. I have homework."

"Suit yourself," Teri says.

The game show cuts to a commercial and there is a loud knock at the door.

"Is there a Mikey bear in there?" shouts a gruff voice.

Mikey squirms out of his mother's lap and races to open the door. My father steps inside.

"Bear!" Mikey squeals.

My father growls and crouches to the ground. Mikey Litch jumps into his arms. They wrestle like grizzlies for a second, both of them laughing, then Dad stands up, holding Mikey. The little bear hands him the ambulance.

"Thank you," Dad says. "Is that ear feeling better? Got a kiss for me?"

Mikey plants a wet one on Dad's cheek and Dad looks at Teri. "Did the medicine help?"

She nods, eyes on the television. "Fever's gone."

"Good evening, Mrs. Litch . . . " His voice trails off.

"Evening, Reverend," Mrs. Litch says.

"Hello, Dad."

You don't see my dad speechless very often. Mikey runs the race car along his shoulder and up his neck. Dad stands there, his eyes locked on me, like he is seeing me for the first time.

Ms. Cummings breaks for the door. "I really have to be going. I have a conference in Troy tomorrow. You'll have a sub, Kate. I hope they dig up a good one. Don't forget to put the chicken in the fridge."

*Bam*—she's gone.

Dad waits until the lights of her Toyota have backed all the way down the driveway before saying anything. "What are you doing here?"

"Teri has my watch."

"Do not," Teri mumbles.

"I want it back."

Teri crosses the room and takes Mikey from my father's arms.

"You know it's mine," I say.

She bounces Mikey up and down on her hip and he clutches at her shirt. "You can't prove it."

"What? How can you say that? Dad, take a look at it."

Rev. Malone frowns and turns off the television. "Kate, this isn't the time. I came here to talk to Mrs. Litch about the fight."

The scar over Mrs. Litch's eye jerks upward. "Another one?"

"Shit," Teri murmurs. She turns and disappears down the dark hall, Mikey still in her arms.

"What about my watch?"

"Did somebody bother you?" her mother calls. "You promised me, Theresa!"

Dad moves a chair in front of the couch and sits. His voice is soft. "I'll explain. It wasn't too bad, but you need to—" He breaks off and looks at me. "Kate, why don't you take that food back to the kitchen?"

Actually, I'd love to sit here and figure out what is going on. Reality feels rather plastic, as if I've been operating in an enclosed sphere, and the covering melted, and all of a sudden I'm in an entirely new world—a world in which my father is tight with the Litches, my chem teacher is a closet social worker, people use lawn tractors for furniture, and watches change hands much too easily.

"Kate," Dad says, a little too loudly. Mrs. Litch sniffs and dabs at her eyes with the edge of her sleeve.

"I'm going."

The kitchen is stuffed into an addition off the back end of the house. The window over the sink gives a terrific view of the rotting barn. Air from the heating vent flutters an old calendar nailed to the wall. Above the small table hangs a plastic clock, frozen at twelve noon. Or midnight, depending on your perspective. One corner of the table is piled high with magazines.

Someone did the dishes earlier. Pale yellow plates and bowls, a couple of coffee cups, and a small plastic mug are upside down in the drainer. They are all dry. The counters are wiped clean.

I put the chicken into the refrigerator and sneak out the back door. I need to run.

# Part 2 | Liquid

$$H_f \; water = 6.0 \; \frac{kJ}{mol}$$

"A catalyst is a substance which increases the rate of a reaction. It is consumed in one step of the reaction and then regenerated later in the process. The catalyst is not used up, but provides a new, lower energy path for the reaction."

—*ARCO Everything You Need to Score High on AP Chemistry,* 3rd Edition

# 3.0 | Galvanize

*SAFETY TIP: Store oxidizers away from other chemicals.*

We have a substitute teacher in chem. He says that we have to watch a movie because chemicals give him a rash and he's really an English teacher. He brought a video from home for us, *Alice in Wonderland*. A family classic, he says.

My lab partner snorts. "Family classic," she mutters. "Mind-altering drugs, demented hatters, and a homicidal queen." She opens her Spanish book to the pluperfect subjunctive.

The movie opens with Alice perched in a tree, complaining about history to her sister. Enter the White Rabbit, stage left, his glasses wobbling at the end of his nose. "I'm overdue, I'm in a stew," he frets.

I sigh and rest my chin on my books. I would not admit this under torture, but I love Disney movies. Everybody does. Disney is our collective stepparent, the nice one who tells us bedtime stories and bakes cupcakes.

Alice follows the rabbit down the hole. She falls, she shrinks, she worms her way past locked doors and winds up a stranger in a strange land with Tweedle-Dee and Tweedle-

Dum blocking her path. They have an eerie Litch-look to them.

I glance at my empty wrist. My watch is still in the clutches of the evil Tweedle-Teri. I borrow Diana's pen and draw a sports watch on my skin. It has a timer, fifty-lap memory, altimeter, barometer, and compass. Alice in Wonderland could use a watch like this. She eats a cookie that is probably laced with human growth hormone and shoots up as big as a house.

I should ask Toby if he's been sneaking Wonderland cookies. That would explain the size of his feet.

There is a soft knock at the door of the classroom. A thin face peers in the window and waves a white envelope at me. It's my father.

Diana looks up from her subjunctives and nudges me.

An envelope. The envelope? An envelope. No, you can't fool me twice. It's too early for the mail. Dad motions for me to join him. Diana pokes my shoulder with her pen. My brain feels like a Slurpee, cold and slow.

Diana shoves me. "Get going, moron."

The sub doesn't notice as I walk across the room. Is it possible to have a heart attack at eighteen? I open the door, step over the threshold, and enter the hall. My father is holding an envelope. The envelope. After all this time, things are happening too fast. I'm not ready. I am going to puke.

"This was stuck in a catalog that came yesterday," Dad says. "You told me to bring it to you." He hands it over. The magic words glow in the upper left-hand corner:

"Massachusetts Institute of Technology, Office of Admissions."

It is a thin envelope.

I open it badly. The envelope tears and rips across my name and address. A jagged opening. The letter is brief, murder by stiletto, a thin, sharp blade: "We regret to inform you . . . thousands of qualified candidates . . . not a reflection on your abilities . . . many opportunities elsewhere . . . Sincerely . . . "

The need to vomit vanishes. Dead girls don't puke.

My father picks up the letter and envelope from the floor. He says something I can't hear. When I don't answer, he looks in the envelope. Maybe the real letter, the acceptance letter, is hidden in there, written in invisible ink on invisible, space-age paper. Or it's a Cheshire cat letter and it will materialize any second now. Somewhere deep in that envelope are my registration instructions, my financial aid package, and a handwritten note from the cross-country coach.

If Dad says that he told me this would happen, I will die all over again.

"I'm sorry," he says. "I'm sorry."

I heard that.

I wish I were three feet tall and he could pick me up and he still had a beard and he wore cotton sweaters that felt soft on my cheek and I could cry it all away and I would wipe my tears on his shoulder and I could suck my thumb and suck the end of my ponytail and he wouldn't tell me only babies did that and he would rock me on the front porch with the wind coming clean from the north and he would sing nursery rhymes with made-up words like Mom used to and he could teach me the alphabet again and how to walk and how to run and maybe I would do it better this time.

Dad clears his throat. "It's not the end of the world, honey. You have all those other schools. Come here. . . . "

He pulls me into a hug. He is wearing the tweed jacket from last night (smells like chicken) and it scratches my cheek. The ground shakes. The iceberg that traps us shifts and groans and I come so close—this close—to being his daughter, the Malone girl, Jack's girl, and letting him be Daddy and love me for all these stupid mistakes, and letting him try to put a Band-Aid on this one even though we both know it's going to bleed for a very long time, but it's the Band-Aid that counts.

I have not inhaled since I saw the envelope. I am inert, an expired reaction.

"You could talk to Mr. Kennedy," he says. "He'll help you choose from the other schools. You have options, honey."

I am so dead that I can't even think about what this means.

"Or I could talk to him. I have a meeting in the guidance department"—he looks at his watch over my shoulder—"in a minute."

I step back, a rush of cold air on my cheeks. "Why?"

He cracks his knuckles. "Mrs. Litch asked me to come. The police are involved because of the fight Teri was in yesterday."

I stand up straighter. "And you thought you'd drop off my letter on the way?"

He frowns. "No, it was more than that. You asked me ... "

The iceberg stops groaning and arctic salt water swirls, restoring the space between us, putting us back in our places.

"I have to get back to chem."

We both look through the door. The cartoon has lulled the class into their happy place. Alice is lost again. Dad folds the letter and inserts it back in the envelope. "We'll talk about this tonight. I know you're upset, but we'll figure something out."

He hugs my head and I hold my breath. I take the envelope and turn my back to him. I step over the threshold, enter the classroom, and close the door behind me, quietly, so it doesn't disturb anyone.

## 3.0.1 ▌ Scientific Method

At my lab table, I review the experiment:

Step 1. Hypothesis—I am brilliant. I am special. I am going to MIT, just like my mom did. I am going to change the world.

Step 2. Procedure—Acquire primary and secondary school education. Follow all rules. Excel at chemistry and math, ace standardized tests. Acquire social skills and athletic prowess; maintain a crushing extracurricular load. Earn

national science fair honors. Apply to MIT. Wait for acceptance letter.

    Step 3. Results—Failure.

    Step 4. Retrace steps. Procedure flawless.

    Step 5. Conclusion—Hypothesis incorrect. I am a loser.
So simple.

    I light the Bunsen burner. The thin envelope goes up in
flames.

## 3.1 ▎ Flammability

Someone has been messing with my locker. 27-18-28.
Jigglejigglejiggle the handle. Locked. 27-18-28. Jigglejigglejiggle. Damn.

    If I weren't trapped in a hall of bodies I could kick this
sucker or punch it or find a chair and smash it against the
crap metal piece of shit until I was standing in a pile of kindling up to my ankles and then the lock would tumble into
place and the handle would jigglejiggle-open. If there
weren't four thousand strangers bumping into me one after
the other, I could get a crowbar and pry this thing open
because I have to get my books and my notebooks and look
at all the stupid crap that is stuck to the inside of my locker
so it can remind me of who I am on days when I forget or
want to forget like this one. If there were any justice in the
world, I'd be able to flatten myself and slide through the

vents in the locker door like Alice in Wonderland, Kate in Wonderland, off with her head!

Try again. 27-18-28.

The humiliation. Searing, scarring humiliation. I can't go to the cafeteria, not ever again. Maybe I could tell them I was banned, that I was caught putting rat poison in the peas or I ran in the hall with scissors. I can't go to English class, either, because Mitch will be there. Come to think of it, I can't ever see him, or Sara, or Travis . . . I can't ever go home, can't go to work . . . kids don't run away to join the circus anymore, do they? Too bad. I could work in the sideshow as Idiot Girl. Or I could run away to New York City and do something dramatically stupid in a subway station.

Jigglejigglejiggle. Why won't this freaking thing open?

I lean my head against the locked locker. The metal draws the heat away from my brain. Everyone assumes I'll go to Syracuse or Ithaca or Drexel, because I applied there, remember? Remember how I sweated over those essays? Remember how I told Dad I wrote the checks for the application fees? Remember how everyone bought the myth that I had been accepted by my safety schools? That I even applied to my safety schools?

The freak show could bill me as the Amazing Lying Egghead. See her bullshit the family! See her lie straight-faced to friends! See her completely tank her life!

If I concentrate hard enough, I should be able to separate the molecules of the metal locker door and melt through the surface. Since the lock is jammed, they'd wouldn't find me until my body had mummified. That would work.

Two hands on my shoulder, a deep voice in my ear: "I've been looking everywhere for you." Mitchell "Harvard Asshole" Pangborn pulls me away from the locker and spins me around. He lifts my chin with his fingers. He can't lift my eyes.

"I know," he says.

"Already?"

"You started a fire in chem class, Malone. Everybody knows."

If I concentrate hard enough, maybe I could separate the molecules of linoleum and wood and steel and concrete beneath my feet and sink slowly into the earth.

"It wasn't a real fire," I say.

"You could have been hurt."

"Ha."

He pulls me into his sweatshirt, and now I have to concentrate not to fall into the spaces between his molecules of skin and muscle and bone. I pull back.

"Don't. I can't be hugged right now. I can't have all this 'It'll be okay' stuff, okay? Don't be nice to me. I'll scream, I swear."

He shoves his hands into the pockets of his jeans. I pull the strap of my photo bag higher on my shoulder and squeeze my books until their edges bite my arms.

"I don't know what to do," he says.

"Join the club. Where's Sara?"

"She's sick. A stomach bug, Travis said."

"She ate Jell-O with nuts last night."

He steps close again, slips his hand around the back of my neck. "Kate."

I shrug him off. "I meant it, Pangborn." I look up, not at his eyes because that would be the end of me, but to glance around the hall. The thousands of bodies have vanished—*poof!* I didn't hear the bell. Somewhere a clock is trying to tick, its hands stuck in molasses.

"I can't open my locker," I say.

He steps around me and spins the dial, 27-18-28. *Click-click-click.* The lock surrenders and the door swings open between us. I throw my books inside and slam it shut.

"I'm late," I say. "I have to go."


## 3.2 | Significant Figure

That crackle you hear? That's the sound of hell freezing over. Alert the media: Kate Malone is ditching class.

The art teacher, Mr. Freeman, and his students are building a statue in the front lobby. The statue is a giant stick figure with two metal legs, a pole for the body, and two long arms thrust in the air. A guy with a skanky mullet is wrapping pâpier-maché around the legs. While the art elves rummage through a half dozen plastic bins filled with junk, the teacher fires up his glue gun.

Artistic people are too random for me, but these kids

look harmless. One girl I recognize. She's half-famous around here: Melinda Something. A senior tried to rape her in a janitor's closet last year. She fought him off and pressed charges, which was cool. It made the papers when he was found guilty. He didn't go to jail, of course. White, upper-middle-class criminals go to the state college, not the state penitentiary. Then they join fraternities.

State college. My future, and only if they have rolling admissions. The nausea starts in my knees and surges upward. I cover my mouth and sink to the floor, my back against the wall. My hands are shaking. They do not feel attached.

**Why I belong at MIT:**
I'm smart.
I work hard.
I aced the math SAT.
I'm a legacy.
I need very little sleep.
I do not require a social life.
Heat and pressure improve my performance.
I could be the reincarnation of Madame Curie (according to Sara).

**Why MIT blew me off:**
I'm not smart enough.
I do not work hard enough.

My verbal SAT was less than perfect.

Mom didn't leave MIT any money in her will.

I scared the admissions officer during my interview.

My essays sucked.

I'm linear, not well-rounded.

I'm too short.


Melinda Something heard me moan. She puts down a spool of copper wire and walks over to where I'm squatting. "Are you okay?"

I nod. She's a sophomore and would not understand the stress of losing your college. I point at the statue. "What's that?"

"Mr. Freeman calls it *Student Body*."

"It looks like a robot."

"It's supposed to be a puppet." She pulls out her scrunchy and combs through her hair with her fingers. "We're covering it with representational pieces, junk that stands for all of us. Freeman keeps telling us, 'Everybody is a piece.' You look really pale. Want me to get the nurse?"

I shake my head. "She can't fix this."

She smoothes her hair back into a ponytail and winds the scrunchy around it. "Got it. Feel free to help, if you want."

"Thanks. I'll just watch."

I watch the puppet grow for the next two periods. They cover it with student council campaign buttons, cheerleader hair ribbons, chess pieces, computer chips, plastic cell phones, excuse cards, a jockstrap and a sports bra (the Student Body is gender-neutral), crayons, erasers, sheet music, and about a million other things. There is an anatomically correct heart glued outside the chest, dark red and shiny. I bet that will be the first thing that gets ripped off. The science geeks are represented by glass test tubes. Worrywart Good Kate wishes they had used plastic.

While they work, I concentrate on alternative career choices. I come up with four.

1. Janitor—I'm great with a toilet brush.

2. Soup kitchen employee—I have significant ladling skills, too.

3. Crack cooker—Drug lords are always looking for good chemists. Except I am terrified of guns. And crack kills brain cells. And Toby would freak out and have the mother of all asthma attacks and . . . Okay, I can't be a crack cooker.

4. Shirt presser—I could work at that little dry-cleaning place next to the Acme.

Gak. Gak. Gak. I think I have a hairball stuck in my throat. Much as it kills me, I'm going to have to talk to my guidance counselor. I stretch once, then stand.

Mr. Freeman chuckles as he works on the sculpture's head, a hornet with monstrous eyes. (Merryweather High is the home of the Fight'n Hornets. It's a long story.) As I leave, the art kids are gluing on hundreds of cutout eyes from the yearbook. All of our eyes together make a kaleidoscope that follows you down the hall. They should call that thing *Frankenstudent*.

## 3.3 | Dissociation

The guidance office is jammed. Picture a mosh pit of enraged parents ready to body-slam the nearest administrator because their Precious Babies did not get into The Right School. These folks have been *robbed*. Do you know how much they pay in taxes?

I wait in line, wait, wait, wait, ignore the choked, snuffling sounds from the Precious Babies curled in the fetal position on plastic orange chairs, ignore the clenched fists, ignore the jiggling knees, the tapping pens. My mind is on pause, my body pulled along by the momentum of the factory line.

When I finally get my turn in front of the secretary, she's on the phone and has ten people on hold. She covers the mouthpiece. "If you're here about a college, Kate, you'll have to take a number." She hands me a pink index card. I am number twenty-seven.

Mr. Kennedy, my guidance counselor, opens his door. "Number four?"

"Come back later, Kate," the secretary suggests. "Or Monday morning, first thing. Do you need a pass?" She scribbles one for me with her left hand. "Go out the back door, hon. It'll be easier."

I shuffle down the hall to the exit, past the sounds of weeping and outrage. The last office is quieter. On one side of the desk sits a guidance counselor. On the other, Teri Litch and her mom, a police officer, and my father. Teri's little brother, Mikey, sits on the floor ripping out pages from a college catalog.

## 3.4 ▌ Calculation

I fumble my way to the math wing. Calculus will save me. Give me integrals, give me functions, derivatives, domains, and ranges. I am a differentially abled student, broken by the text-based world. I stumble into class and open the holy book.

*Consider the problem of finding the limit for the following function when the value of x is greater than 1: lim $100^n$ $n \to \infty$.*

Aaaahhh. I ponder a table of neatly organized values, values of x, values of n, and values of $x^n$.

*As n approaches $\infty$, $x^n$ approaches $\infty$.*

Math reminds me of pebbles, a whole beach of smooth, wet pebbles that you can pick up, turn over, taste, set down. They can be stacked, subtracted, divided, they can be arranged into patterns, into forms, into meaning. As I do the math, my blood pressure returns to normal. My stomach stops pumping sulfuric acid. My neck unspazzes.

I finish the problem set before anyone else. Our Math God, Mr. Dodgson, is in the back helping someone who is struggling with the theory of limits. Duh. Next set: *lim/x $\to$ $\infty$ $x^2 + 1/2x - 3$.* And so on, and so on, into infinity. Pondering infinity for me might be what prayer is for other people.

*Prayer . . . church . . . Dad . . . letter (thin) . . . rejection + destruction of life dream = utter misery.*

Oh, crap.

Time for a clean page. I need to break down my real-life limit problem into its component parts; analyze it, turn it over, taste it; look for the pattern, the form, the meaning. Dissolve the granules of a problem in imagination and come up with a solution.

Goal—get into MIT.

Obstacle—they don't want me.

Solution—x . . .

Maybe I could leak this news to the newspaper and shame MIT into letting me in. Maybe I could write to all their famous chemistry grads and get them to force the university to let me in. Maybe I could send them pictures of my father and then they would feel so sorry for me they would let me in. I could offer to work in food service. I could be a probationary student. I could pledge them my first million dollars in wages, and patents to any world-changing discoveries I make. I could name a new element massachusetts-institutumtechnologium.

Good Kate whispers that maybe, perhaps, there could be a small chance that I need to suck it up and accept the situation.

I would rather fall down a bottomless hole.

■   ■   ■

Mitch is lurking in the hall when I leave calc. He follows me. His mouth is moving. Again.

"Look, Kate. It's not like the world has ended. They can't take all the geniuses that apply. But it's going to be okay. I just think you should . . . will you at least look at me? Kate? You have to talk about it. This is stupid. Come back. Come on, Malone . . . Kate!"

The guidance secretary tells me that my counselor had to drive a girl to the hospital. She fainted and cracked her forehead on the edge of his desk. Georgetown rejected her. Stitches, for sure.

The adults in this place need better math skills. Merryweather High has more than one thousand seniors. Eighty percent applied to college. College rejections arrive the same week that fall schedules have to be filled out. We have a total of four guidance counselors.

That is what we call an imbalanced equation, class.

Mitch is waiting for me outside French. I worm my way into a gaggle of giggling freshman and sneak past him.

## 3.5 ▍Iron

When the final bell rings, I scurry along the back halls to the locker room. I need to run until I bleed, run all the fluids out of my body, pound, pound the road, unplug the hardware, destroy the system. Right now I could run a marathon and worship every step.

So, of course, Coach Reid declares that today we're conditioning in the weight room. He unlocks the door and directs people to the silver instruments of torture: lat pulldown, biceps curl, leg extension. He hesitates when he gets to me. I'm a graduating senior and there are thunderclouds gathered above my head.

"All right, Malone. You get a treadmill," Coach says. "Don't slack."

No, sir. I step onto the middle treadmill and punch in a flat course, 3.1 miles, a six-minute-mile pace. Forget about a slow, safe warm-up. I want to feel it.

The room heats up quickly. The radio is badly tuned to a metal station. Weights clang against one another, athletes grunt and strain. The stair-steppers grind, *whnrr-whnrr-whnrr.* The girls on the steppers keep their hands on their hips and their chins up. The guys on the other treadmills try to match my pace.

Oh, yeah?

I crank it up another notch. I streak through a half mile, my sneakers blistering the rubber belt. The guy to my right can't hack it. He backs off, slows down. The guy to my left has sweat dripping down his cheek. He's holding his left elbow against his side. I chuckle.

Coach Reid is helping a sophomore bench-press twelve

pounds. "Stop showing off, Malone," he shouts.

Bad Kate hopes the sophomore drops that weight on Coach's foot. Good Kate is frantically pointing to our tender Achilles tendon. I know I can run faster than this. I take it higher. My sneakers squeak, sounding like tiny voices on helium: "*brrp . . . brrrpp . . .* messed-up . . . screwed-up . . . messed-up . . . screwed-up."

The guy on my left gives in to his cramps and decelerates. Wussy boy.

"Slow it down, Malone," Coach orders.

The sneaker voices move up off the belt and whisper that they are disappointed in me, that I'm stupid, that I should be ashamed of myself, young lady. Run faster, Kate. Just a little faster, push it.

I am flying, whipping through the air. The faces around me blur. My right knee sends up a warning signal, my Achilles is screaming. I can feel the fibers in my quads fraying. Give me the pain, bring it. I want my heart to explode, a bruised cherry smashed deep in my chest. The muscles under my ribs seize up. I think my shirt is on fire.

"Kate. Kate. Kate. Kate." I don't know who is saying that. How can they be standing still when I'm running so damn fast?

"Look out, Kate!" Another voice, fading away. Another ghost.

The lights flicker. Coach Reid yells in my ear, but I can't hear him. His hand slams the red STOP button.

■   ■   ■

## 3.5.1 ▌ Rust

Okay, so I might have passed out a little bit when they dragged me off the treadmill. I just needed a nap. A nap, some dinner, and a shower. No big deal. Just leave me alone.

## 3.6 ▌ Dissolve

When I get home, I park Bert by the front door and don't bother to carry any books inside. I brush past Toby in the front hall.

"Don't say a word," I warn. "I'm not here. You don't see me."

He nods. "You're not here. I don't see you. Well, when you show up, I'll tell you that Sara and Mitch keep calling. They sound desperate." He shoves a handful of Chee·tos in his mouth. "Did you break up with him or something?"

"Don't eat all of those."

I lock the bathroom door, strip, and step into the shower. We have hot water again, thanks to Mr. Lockheart and his magic tools. Boiling, scalding, sterilizing water hurts so good. I close my eyes and let it fall on my head. It slips off me as if I were covered in oil.

I lather up. Soap: $C_{15}H_{31}CO_2Na$. Long molecules designed to suck up dirt, sweat, and humiliation. Rinse, lather, rinse, lather, rinse until the soap melts down to a waxy crescent that jumps out of my hand.

I know I should think about MIT, be logical, be practical, but I can't get my brain started. It needs jumper cables. Given my mood, I'd hook them up the wrong way. Little mistake, big consequences. *Boom*, there goes the brain, the engine, the college application.

*Boom . . . a mistake. What if they made a mistake?*

It happens, even at the best schools. A clerical error. Or the computer messed up. *A mistake.* It happens. Two kids with the same name apply—one is accepted, the other gets the boot, but the letters are switched. The wrong Kate Malone got into MIT. *It was all a mistake.*

Wait until I tell them!

I can see the future play out like a movie on the shower curtain. I'll drive to MIT and talk to the admissions officer. When she hears about my rejection she'll freak and say, "You poor thing! Of course we want you!" She'll fire her assistant and type up my acceptance letter with her own fingers. She'll hand me the fat envelope loaded with goodies. Maybe I'll get more financial aid or a choice dorm room.

I am so excited I soap up my left leg and grab the razor. This is going to work. Toby pounds on the bathroom door and yells something I can't hear. I shave my kneecap and ignore him. He can pee downstairs.

Details, details: MIT is approximately 301 miles to the east, a six-hour drive. I'll have to leave before dawn. What should I bring? Copies of my transcript and two scientific papers, for sure. Maybe I should leave my essay home. That was definitely weak. I loathe essays. No—I'll bring it. It will prove I know my strengths and weaknesses. I will even admit that I need to improve my writing skills. My molecular models? I pull the razor along my calf, leaving a smooth runway of skin in its wake. I rinse off the blade. No, don't bring the models. That would look desperate.

I lather my foot and shave my hairy toes. I don't want to look like a hobbit. Toby pounds on the door and hollers again. It doesn't sound like he's speaking English.

"Go away!" I yell.

I rinse off the razor and twist around to shave the back of my ankle. Toby beats on the door just as the blade slides over my Achilles tendon. I flinch and the razor nicks me. It takes a second for the blood to flow.

"I'm not opening it!"

Silence. Good.

I work on my right leg and concentrate on the plan. There are a few kinks to work out. Bert won't survive the drive. He can barely make it to the grocery store. I'll need to borrow a car. And find some cash. And get an appointment. But it's going to work. I'll make it work.

I shave my right leg without a single nick or cut. That is truly a sign from God. I turn off the water and reach for a towel. My hair is clean, my legs are sleek, and I don't have hobbit toes. MIT will let me in. I am ready for the world.

Toby is waiting when I open the door. He barges in and yanks on the bathroom blinds.

"What are you doing?" I ask.

"Look." He wipes the steam off the window with his

sleeve and points to the red-orange glow down the hill.

Oh. My. God.

"That's what I was trying to tell you, butthead."

The Litches' barn is on fire, a roaring furnace. The trees in the side yard are blazing torches; rogue flames lick the roof of the house. Three fire trucks are on the scene, cherry lights pulsing beneath the smoke, firefighters wrestling thick hoses in the  shadows.

"Are they okay?" I whisper.

The wind kicks up and the fire blooms.

"The Litches? Yeah. They're downstairs."

## 3.7 ▎ Effective Collision

I sit down hard on the toilet seat, clutching the towel around me.

"The Litches are here?"

"Not the mom. Just Teri and her little brother."

There is a quiet knock on the door. "May I come in?"

Dad enters before I can answer. His eyes are bright, fueled by alarm bells and emergency flashers. His sweater reeks of smoke.

"We need to talk." He closes the door behind him and locks it.

"Can it wait until I'm wearing clothes?" I ask.

"This will just take a second. Teri and Mikey are sleeping here tonight. Teri can bunk with Kate. Mikey will stay with you, Toby."

No, he didn't really say that. No way. I must have steam in my ears, or I banged my head when I passed out. That would explain this nausea, too. Maybe I have a concussion.

"Aw, Dad," Toby whines.

Dad raises the lecture finger. "No complaining. They are our neighbors and they are in need."

Teri Litch in my house, in my bedroom. She'll murder me in my sleep with an ax. I'm going to hurl. I scoot off the toilet onto the floor and raise the seat.

"Why can't he sleep in your room?" Toby says.

"You're younger, he'll be more comfortable with you," Dad says. "Besides, I've got to get back to the fire."

Please, let me hurl. Please, please, please.

"Are you sick, honey?"

No such luck. I am just a wet girl in a towel inspecting the rim of the toilet, and it is disgusting.

"What about their mom?" Toby asks. "Shouldn't they be with her?"

"The doctor said she needs some quiet. A lot of quiet. She's going to stay at Betty's house until we get things sorted out."

"Somebody better warn her about Jesus living in Betty's television," I say. "Can't they go to the Red Cross?"

"Kate, that's absurd. We have plenty of room."

"How long do they have to stay?" Toby asks.

"A week, maybe."

I choke, cough, and lean over the toilet again.

"We'll know more in the morning. Are you sure you're okay?" Dad asks.

"I'm not staying here if she's going to barf," Toby says.

The snap of the door closing behind him echoes off the tile and porcelain. I sigh, close the toilet lid, and get back to my feet, adjusting the towel for some dignity. My father leans against the sink, watching me closely. Emotion won't help here. I sit on the toilet and cross my legs.

"Okay, Dad. Let's face facts. There are a number of reasons why this won't work. One: Teri Litch is a psychopath. Remember how she used to beat me up?"

"I know you two are not exactly friends—"

"Two: This house is not ready for a toddler. Who is going to take care of Mikey during the day? Three: Teri is a thief. She stole my watch, remember? Mom's old watch that I have worn forever? Four—"

"Four," he interrupts. "You've had a terrible day. I know I'm asking a lot, and I promise, we'll make time—just you and me—to sit down this weekend and go over all your material, so when you to school on Monday, you can tell people which college you chose. It won't be MIT, but trust me, no one will care."

The nausea is back.

Toby knocks on the door. "Dad?" he says. "Some ladies are here with casseroles and diapers."

■  ■  ■

The family room smells like smoke and sounds like a stadium. Teri Litch is sprawled across the couch, remote in one hand, a can of soda in the other, watching baseball. Sophia is curled up next to her, close but not touching. She doesn't even look at me. Mr. Spock thumps his tail once and lifts his head, his eyebrows raised high. He'd love to come and slobber on me, but he's busy being a pillow for Teri's little brother, who is resting his head on the dog's stomach. Mikey is pale, with smudges of soot on his cheeks. His eyes are puffy from crying and he's sucking his thumb. His other hand is holding a green metal motorcycle.

The dog drops his head back to the ground with a sigh. Mikey looks up at me with a watery smile. His upper lip quivers around his thumb as he tries not to cry. He needs to blow his nose.

I am such a pig.

Good Kate shoves Bad Kate out of the way. There are boxes of donated clothes over in the church; it'll be easy to find something for the Litches to wear. They need to shower, and some hot chocolate would be just the thing. I bet Toby's old teddy bear is in the attic somewhere; Mikey might like that. Poor little guy. And I won't confront Teri about the watch, not tonight, not even tomorrow.

(Bad Kate gets up and dusts herself off. She notes that a crisis in our back yard will do a good job distracting Dad while I sort out the MIT mess-up. She walks off into the night, whistling.)

"I'm sorry about the fire," I say.

Teri scratches Sophia's head. The cat doesn't care. She's focused on the game. The Yankees are beating the Indians, 6–3.

"We have some clothes that will fit Mikey," I continue. "I'll find some stuff for you, too."

Teri points the remote and turns up the volume.

*Mmmbbraaaaaaaacchhh . . .*

Teri gave Mikey a bath during the seventh-inning stretch. He fell asleep on my bed while she showered and changed into some of Dad's old sweats. I suggested we move Mikey to the cot in Toby's room, but Teri refused. Can't say I blame her. The dog won't sleep in there, either.

*Braaaaaaaacccchhhhh . . .*

It wasn't part of my plan to be the schmuck that wound up on the cot, but there you go. Teri and Mikey took my bed. As if worrying about MIT weren't enough to keep me awake, I have a lawn mower roaring in the middle of the room.

*Mmmbrrrraaaaachhhhh . . .*

The lawn mower is Mikey Litch breathing through his mouth, producing a decibel-per-pound output that is off the charts. I should sample the noise and sell it to struggling musicians. I'd make a fortune.

*Braaaaaaaacccchhh.*

I roll over and pull my knees up to my chest. My legs are tight, my arms are achy, and I can't get warm. I bet I'm getting the flu. Maybe I'll be lucky and it will be a rare strain from Mongolian hamsters and I'll die. No, I'm not that lucky.

If I got Mongolian hamster flu, I'd probably end up with per-manent blue spots and a tail or something. I roll over. Everything smells like smoke.

*Braaaaaaacccchhh.*

How can Teri stand it? This could explain her anger management problem. I've got to do something or I'll never get to sleep. Maybe I can roll him on his side. I sit up. Teri's shape lies along the edge of the mattress. Her face is blocked by my clock radio. Is she asleep? I sit up higher.

She's awake, watching the minutes on the face of the clock dissolve into each other. The cot creaks under me.

Teri's eyes swivel and pin me to the wall.

# 4.0 | Oxidizing Agent

*SAFETY TIP: Substitute plastic labware for glassware when possible.*

First thought upon waking: Maybe it was a nightmare.

Second thought upon waking: What in God's name is that awful smell?

Third thought: The nightmare continues.

I wrestle my way out of the sleeping bag, fumble for my glasses, and stand up. Mikey Litch's diaper has exploded all over my bed. Believe me, I do not freak out about a little baby poop. I have a brother. Poop, puke, whatever, I can cope. But this is not natural. It looks like a dinosaur took a dump.

Mikey's eyes flutter and open. He turns his head to stare at me. "Where Mommy?"

"Don't move. I, um, I'll get help. Don't move, Mikey, stay. Sit. Stay."

"Twuck," Mikey says, reaching for the toy on the pillow next to him.

"Dad!" I bellow. "Daaad!" Mr. Spock gallops up the stairs, streaks into the room, and freezes, his nose high in the air. He takes a sniff, whimpers, and scurries out, tail between his legs.

Toby takes the stairs two at a time. "What's wrong?"

I point to the bed. Mikey is running the dump truck (oh, irony) over the hills and valleys of my ruined comforter, buzzing his lips to make a spluttering engine noise.

"Dude," Toby says. He backs away from the door and coughs. "That's a lot of—"

"Please don't say it. Where's Teri?"

"Watching cartoons."

Mikey crawls to the edge of the bed. "Oh, no, you don't." I run in and shoo him to the middle of the mattress like a baby herder. "I have to go to work," I tell my brother. "Do something."

"No way, I'm not touching him. That's sick."

"Get Teri."

Toby nods. "Good idea." He turns his head and yells, "*Teri!*"

"I could have done that."

"Yeah, but you didn't."

Teri lumbers up the steps chewing something. Her sweatpants are covered with cat fur. She catches a whiff and shakes her head. "Oh, geez," she says to no one in particular. "He did it again." She tucks Mikey under her arm like a football and carries him downstairs to the kitchen. As she passes me, I notice a thin gold chain disappearing under the collar of her shirt. I know that chain. There is a gold heart attached to it. It was a Christmas present from Mitch.

Toby and I open all the windows in my room, then follow them. "What if she puts him on the couch?" he whispers.

"Who cares? See that necklace she's wearing? It's mine. She stole it."

"For real?"

"For real."

He picks up and shakes the box of Life cereal that Teri left on the couch. It's empty. "What are you going to do?"

"I'm thinking."

"Good idea."

Mikey stands naked and shivering in the kitchen sink, his thumb in his mouth. Teri pulls the spray nozzle out of the faucet and tests the water temperature on the inside of her right wrist before hosing off the first layer of crud and lathering him up with dishwashing detergent.

"Did you get any sleep?" I ask.

Teri slides her hands across Mikey's shoulders and back. Her palms are callused and the thumbnail of her left hand is black. "Not much," she says.

I open the cupboard and get out Toby's medicine and vitamins. "He sure can snore, can't he?"

"He's been sick. His nose is stuffed."

Bubbles cover Mikey's skinny body like translucent polar bear fur. As he bounces up and down, some of them drift off and hang in the sunlight. One lands on the purple bruise under Teri's eye. Mikey pops it and giggles. Teri winces (that must have hurt), then rinses him off.

I pour two glasses of orange juice and set one in front of my brother, sitting at the kitchen table. "Do you want some juice?" I ask Teri as I stick a piece of bread in the toaster.

"I hate juice," she says.

"What about Mikey?"

"He only drinks grape juice."

"Sorry, we don't have any."

"Figures."

I keep my lips pressed together until my toast springs up. "What does he like to eat for breakfast?"

"Cereal."

"That's all gone," Toby points out.

I spread a thin layer of butter on my toast. "How about eggs?"

"He hates eggs."

"Toast?"

Teri pulls fifty paper towels off the roll. "We only eat cereal for breakfast. Or oatmeal, if it's cold outside." She glares at me, daring me to criticize oatmeal. "You need to go to the grocery store."

"Dad'll go." I look down at my wrist—no watch, duh—check the kitchen clock. "Shoot. I have to hurry."

"Um, Kate?" Toby's voice cracks a little.

"So what—we're supposed to starve?" Teri asks.

I open the refrigerator. "Milk, bread, stuff for salad, leftover meatloaf, bologna, cottage cheese, apples, and oranges; there's plenty to eat."

Teri dries off the soles of Mikey's feet. "I knew it. I told your father you didn't want us here."

Deep-breathe, Malone. Count to ten. "I'm going upstairs

to get dressed and then I am going to work. Have a nice day, Teri."

"Kate, listen," Toby starts.

"What?"

"You don't have to go to work."

I pause in the doorway and turn around. "Yes, I do. I'm scheduled all day, then I'm getting my contacts. It's on the calendar."

"Um, well, Dad called your boss, before you woke up," he says. "He said you couldn't go in, that we had an emergency and you had to help at home."

"What emergency?"

Teri smiles as Mikey leaps into her arms. "Me," she says.


## 4.1 ▌ Unstable Compound

I know the Bible says it's wrong to kill your dad, but the Bible says lots of things we ignore these days.

I bang out of the back door in my pajamas and slippers and stalk around the cemetery. I am vibrating at such a high frequency that dogs are howling in Buffalo. I can't believe he did this. He's going to get me fired, and for what—so I can baby-sit a burned-out kleptomaniac whose brother has intestinal issues? I don't think so.

The Litch place is crawling with people: police, firefighters, construction workers, and a half dozen gawkers clustered in the side yard. The barn is a charred skeleton of timbers and half a wall. The house looks all right, though. It has some holes in the roof, but they are already covered with blue tarps. The back porch and half the kitchen burned away, but the rest is standing. Good. She can move out this afternoon.

Dad is leaning against the Dumpster in the driveway, surrounded by guys in hard hats. He's dressed for action—heavy-duty jeans, ancient boots, thick work gloves—and buzzing on adrenaline. (Rev. Malone is most alive when someone is dead, dying, or in trouble. This is item #1342 on the list of things I don't understand about my father. )

The wind picks up as I walk down the hill. The barn timbers shudder. Ghostly whirlwinds of ash rise and writhe over the crowd, and the people turn their faces away so they don't breathe it in.

I plant myself in front of my father. "Are you trying to get me fired?"

Dad blinks. "Gentlemen, this is my daughter, Kate."

The hard hats make polite noises.

"You had no right to call my boss like that."

He won't look me in the eye. "We'll talk about it later. How are our guests?"

"Hungry. When are they leaving?"

"Um, Pete?" Dad nods to one of the men.

Pete pushes up his hard hat with the back of his hand. "Well, the inspector is still poking around. The roof needs patching, and the kitchen here, that's gotta come down and be rebuilt. We got lots of water damage and smoke. But the foundation's in great shape."

"Can they move back in today? After you clean it up?"
I ask.

The men shake their heads slowly.

"A week?"

"Well, like I said, the inspector makes the decisions. Plus your father, he has an idea about rebuilding everything."

The wind gusts, blowing my pajama pants against my legs and making the bones of the barn creak. Bad. Bad. It's bad when Dad has ideas. There was the year he decided Christmas was not about gift-giving and almost started a riot at the mall. . . .

Dad smacks his hands together and grins. "The doctors told me that Mrs. Litch needs some rest. The scare last night didn't do her heart any good. I had a nice chat with her early this morning. I told her all about my idea and she loved it. Gave me full permission."

Then there was the year he told the newspapers that Easter was for fasting, not for eating chocolate. Our house got egged for that one.

"What's the idea?" I ask.

"I told Mrs. Litch about the Amish."

The image of Teri Litch dressed as an Amish girl makes me dizzy. I grab my father's arm. "Please, Dad."

He pats my hand and grins wider. "The Amish can build an entire barn in a day. We can do something like that if we just pull together. The church is going to provide volunteers and the money to fix up the Litch house. It's faith in action, my friends, faith in action!"

The guys in hard hats squirm as if they have an itch they can't reach. People would like my dad better if he weren't always bringing up the religion thing.

I pull my hands away. "Okay, that's great, but how long does Teri have to stay with us?"

"It depends on what we find inside," Pete says. "Weeks. Months, maybe."

Before I can scream or bash my head against the Dumpster, one of the hard hats hollers toward the house. "Hey! You can't go in there!"

Teri Litch is about to blow. With Mikey riding on her back, she strides onto the side porch and rips down the yellow caution tape strung across the door. Mikey giggles. The barn shivers.

Two cops join her on the porch. Teri sets down Mikey and faces them with her fists clenched.

"Do something, Dad," I say.

As my father sprints over to play peace negotiator, Teri lets fly with an astounding collection of profanity, delivered at full volume. To paraphrase: "Get out of my way, you *adjective noun*. This is my *multiple adjective* house, and none of you *plural noun* belong here." She points at the volunteers staring at her. (More paraphrasing here.) "I want you to arrest these *adverb, adverb, truly rude gerund* mothers. They're trespassing. Get them out!"

My father speaks to her in a low voice. I doubt he's cursing. I must admit there is a part of me that would give anything to be able to swear like that in front of a group of strangers.

Mikey toddles down the porch steps. Teri interrupts my father to scream at me. "Dammit, Kate, get him!"

Everybody in this soap-opera trailer-park nightmare turns to look at me. I stumble after Mikey (it was a bad idea to come down here in slippers), scoop him up, and sniff cautiously. He smells like dishwashing detergent. He leans back in my arms and gives me the once-over. "I'm Kate," I say. "Can you say 'Kate'?"

"Twuck," Mikey says, showing me the dump truck in his hand.

"Kate." I point to myself.

"Twuck." He shoves the truck in my face.

"Close enough."

Mikey and I sit down on the grass, far away from the remains of the barn. The way the wind is blowing, it's going to come down soon. Dad must have achieved détente. He follows Teri inside the house, accompanied by a police officer.

Mikey runs his truck over the grass and my slipper. What the hell am I doing here, having an out-of-body experience? I should be shopping for a microwave for my dorm room, or talking to Sara, or at the very least earning some cash so I can pay for my books and . . . "No, no, don't eat that!" I pull Mikey into my lap and clean the grass out of his mouth. "Yucky, uck."

"Uck," he repeats.

"Precisely. A category-three uck."

"Free." He scrunches up his face and wipes his tongue.

"How did you get so cute?" Teri dressed him in overalls

and a red flannel shirt that belonged to Toby when he was a rugrat. I need to distract him. "Come here, I'll teach you something." I set him in front of me and pull his palms together. "It's like patty-cake, only better because it has chemistry."

"Uck."

"No, not uck. Give it a shot. You'll love it." I clap his hands in mine and sing, "There's antimony, arsenic, aluminum, selenium, and hydrogen and oxygen and nitrogen and rhenium . . . "

The boy is not so sure about this. The Litches have neglected his education.

"No, wait. It gets better. And nickel, neodymium, neptunium, germanium . . . hey, what are you doing?"

"Uck." Mikey pulls his hands away, stands up. "Up." He stretches his arms over his head.

I pick him up and settle him on my hip. He rests his head against my shoulder, thumb in his mouth. I sway back and forth. What does he think about all this? His mom gone, his sister . . . well, I guess he's used to her. Maybe Mikey could stay with us for a while. He could go to the preschool at church. Dad obviously likes him. He could stay with us while Mrs. Litch gets her life back together. Between the three of us, we could take care of him, just for a while.

Teri comes out of the house carrying a black garbage bag and a basket of toys. Mikey scrambles out of my arms and runs to her. Dad follows with another bag. A teddy bear pokes out the top of it. The cop refastens the the yellow caution tape across the door.

Teri puts the toy basket on the ground for Mikey.

"Is everything okay?" I ask.

"Kind of." The wind grabs her hair and tangles it.

Dad sets down his bag. "I explained the situation. Mrs. Litch hadn't had the chance to tell Teri about this. I assumed she had. My fault."

Teri picks up the teddy bear, sniffs it, then holds it out to me. "Can you smell smoke on this?"

I sniff. "Yeah."

"Damn."

I check the tag sewn into the bear's foot. "We can wash it at our house. I have a lot of laundry to do."

Mikey finds what he was looking for in the basket. "Twuck," he crows, waving his fire truck in the air. "Woo-woo-woo!" It's a pretty good siren imitation.

"You have to go grocery shopping, too," Teri reminds me.

The police have started to push people away from the barn. It's ready to topple. Dad watches the crowd move backward and sighs.

"If you want to go to work, Kate, that would be fine," he says. "We don't need you here. It'll be all right."

I nod. Mikey drives his fire truck over my slipper. The wind runs over the new grass.

"They've already called someone in to take my shift," I say.

"No, really," Dad says. "The volunteers will be here soon. One of them can take Teri on her errands. You've got a lot to do. Plus, we have to talk about the college thing. We could do that at lunch."

I crouch down to gather the metal cars and trucks. "Don't worry about it. I can take her. Mikey, too, if we can find a car seat."

Teri raises an eyebrow. "You're driving me around? Not in those pajamas, you're not."

The wind gusts hard and the crowd watching it steps farther back. The barn shakes once, then collapses. The timbers scatter on the ground like pickup sticks.

## 4.2 ▌ Neutralization

Before we leave, I refill Bert's radiator and give him a friendly pat. *Don't let me down, buddy. We do not want to be stranded with these passengers.*

The engine starts the first time. Teri rolls down her window and fiddles with the radio as I wind my way to the main road. She taps the bumper sticker on my dashboard. "So, this MIT, it's like a big deal, huh? A brainiac school?" she asks.

I nod once, eyes ahead. "It's the best, the very best." Mikey throws a truck at the back of my seat.

Teri chuckles. "You think I never heard of MIT? Duh. I'm not retarded, you know."

"Let's not talk about MIT right now, okay?"

She sits back. "Your dad said they blew you off. He didn't

want me to think you were being a bitch because you didn't like me or anything."

"My father is a very sensitive man. Here, this is Betty's house."

Teri and Mikey spend half an hour closed in the bedroom where Mrs. Litch is "recuperating." Betty serves me tea and orange bundt cake and gives me the 411 about Mrs. Litch's "conditions." She has a number of them, apparently. At least Betty doesn't bug me about college.

A door slams. Teri strides through the kitchen without a word, dragging Mikey behind her. I guess that's her way of saying we can leave now.

Mikey is already buckled into his car seat by the time I get outside.

"Hurry up," Teri says.

I start the car, buckle my belt, and reverse. "How's your mother?"

She flips the door lock up, down, up, down. "Coughing a little. Whining a lot."

"Is she excited about the house getting fixed?"

Up, down. Up, down. Up, down.

All right, don't answer me. I look in the rearview mirror. Mikey is watching the traffic, his thumb in his mouth.

Up, down. Up, down.

"Knock it off," I say. "This car is a collector's item."

Up, down.

I try again. "Is she still upset about the fire? Does she want you and Mikey to stay with her?"

"Okay, listen up, *Katie*. My mom got hit in the head with a bat once. My dad was holding the bat. Mom gets confused. She doesn't understand what's going on with the house. Hell, she thinks old Betty there is a cousin. I don't want to talk about her anymore."

Up, down. Up, down. Up, down. Up, down.

"I'm sorry," I say.

Up, down. "I gotta get paid. Take a left."

Getting paid means a visit to The Moon, a biker bar on the lake. The owner pays Teri in cash, and I don't have the guts to ask what kind of work she does for him. I'm just the driver. It's a lot of money, though.

What do you do after you get paid? You might think you would go to the bank. But not if you were Teri Litch. We go to Burgerbarf, where Teri and Mikey get jumbo-sized orders of french fries, soda, and cheeseburgers. Then I drive to the car wash so I can clean the jumbo soda Mikey spilled in the back. Then we go back to Burgerbarf for more fries. I drive them to the mall and stay in the car watching Bert's temperature gauge. When they come out, Teri is holding a plain white bag, and Mikey is holding a strawberry ice cream cone. The cone is upside down on the seat before we leave the parking lot. She should never have gotten him a double scoop. Poor little guy. We revisit the car wash.

When the seat is clean, I take a detour by the pharmacy so I can apologize, grovel, and beg to keep my job. After that, my afternoon on chauffeur duty crawls by at twenty-five miles an hour. Teri pays her family's water bill and electric bill with cash. She spends forever in the social services office arguing about a check Mikey is supposed to be getting. After that, she's on a rampage. She starts up a running monologue mocking my car, complaining about my driving, and bitching about the fire. Mikey throws cold french fries at my head, then falls asleep. I turn off the radio and Teri goes silent, watching the stores and the streets slip by.

"I have to pick up my contacts now," I say. No response. I check the mirror, get in the left lane, and turn when the green arrow flashes. "You can stay in the car if you want. It shouldn't take long."

She turns around to check on Mikey. "He's out cold. He'll sleep."

I drive down the boulevard a few more blocks, then pull into the shopping center. I park in front of Ocu-Brite.

"You know how to use a hammer?" Teri asks as I open my door.

"What?" I drop my keys in my purse.

"Can you hammer things? Nails. Or are you a total spaz?" She snorts and turns to the window again. "Forget it. Go on. You're a spaz. I shoulda known."

"No, open the eyelid wider, wider, that's it, nice and big. Right. Now, keep the contact on the tip of your finger, ease it onto your eyeball, and . . . No. You have very dry eyes, don't you? Let's try some artificial tears."

Ocu-Brite's official contact trainer is dressed like a medical person: white coat with big pockets, serious glasses, pager at her belt. It's all bogus. She used to be a grocery store cashier. I can't figure out if teaching people to poke themselves in the eye at Ocu-Brite is a step up or a step down on the job scale.

"One more time," the trainer says. "Deep breath."

I take a deep breath and study my eyeball. In the magnifying mirror, it's as big as a grapefruit, with bright red capillaries snaking away from the pupil. I have Medusa eyes, and they are battling the contacts.

As I peel back my eyelid, the bell on the front door jingles. Teri and Mikey toddle in.

"Can I help you?" the contact trainer asks.

"I doubt that," Teri says. She sits next to me and looks in the magnifying mirror. "Dang, look at your nostrils! And you've got a zit getting ready to pop out. Right there, on your chin."

I push the mirror away. "Why didn't you stay in the car?" I ask.

"Mikey's awake."

Mikey shoves a pile of magazines on the floor before running to the far end of the store.

"Hurry up," Teri tells me.

Like she's in any kind of position to be ordering me around. Like she hasn't already messed up my day enough, plus my night when you figure I got about three hours of sleep.

"Let's try this one more time," the trainer says.

Teri sits in a waiting room chair and Mikey jumps into her lap. She reads him a copy of *This Old House* magazine. The little guy settles in and listens to the benefits of proper insulation. He is clutching a pair of demo frames in his fist.

*Pop!* The contact snuggles up against my eyeball.

"It's in! It's in!"

"Congratulations," drones the trainer. "Follow me."

At the counter, she rattles off a list of instructions and stuffs a paper bag with freebie contact junk. Then she hands me the bill. I take out my wallet and remove the faded twenties. She takes my money. It's that simple. I pay, I can see. Next customer.

I walk out of the store and clutch a concrete post. The light is blinding, screaming off the windshields and the metal cars, amplified by the white stucco walls of the shopping center. Water gushes from my eyes. Not tears, just water, eye water.

After a couple of minutes the water level goes down, and I can open my eyes, a little. If I block out the sun with my hand it's not so bad. Holy crap, I can see *everything:* the numbers on the license plates, the small print on the signs in the music store window, the price of gas at the Sunoco. (Yikes, when did that go up?) I can see the street signs. I can see cardinals flying. I can see the cardinal's beak, the twig in the cardinal's beak, the flash in the cardinal's eye.

*Laurie Halse Anderson*

I have magic eyes.

The bell jingles again and Teri and Mikey strut out of Ocu-Brite. Mikey is wearing the stolen frames and Teri is carrying the issue of *This Old House*. I can see the ice cream stain on his shirt and the scar under her chin. I follow them to the car, squinting from the intense light, captivated by the exquisite details of our little strip mall. The dust caught in the petal of a buttercup growing in a crack in the sidewalk. The weary faces of the teenagers working at the video store. A woman walks by carrying a briefcase. Her nails are bitten and torn. I can see them. A family bounces out of the sports equipment store carrying a huge rubber raft. I can see the price tag. They paid too much.

## 4.3 ▌ Free Radicals

Just a few normal hours, that's all I wanted. I drove Teri and Mikey back to our house. I made hamburgers and mashed potatoes, and Toby made salad. At that point, I figured I was off the hook. Since I was avoiding my friends, I figured I could hide in a movie theater for a few hours. At the very least, I figured Teri was going to put Mikey to bed and watch television. And leave me alone.

That, my friends, is what they call hubris. Dad asked me to get out my acceptance letters and course catalogs. Teri bitched about the lack of grape juice and oatmeal. It was a no-brainer. Off to the grocery store we go.

■ ■ ■

As the Superfresh doors glide open, I rip the shopping list in two and hand half of it to Teri. "I'll meet you at the checkout counter," I say. "And don't get any junk, okay? I don't have much cash."

Teri shoves the list in her back pocket without looking at it, takes a shopping cart, and wheels away without a word. I head for the produce aisle, where my best friend in the universe (whom I am avoiding like the plague) is squeezing pomegrantes. Shoot. She spots me before I can duck behind the display of grapes.

"Oh ma gah, Kate!" Sara drops the fruit and runs over to hug me. "I've called you like ten million times. Your dad said you hadn't started any more fires or anything, but Kate, damn, how are you?" She squeezes me again and pats me on the back. "I am soooo sorry. They should have let you in. They are morons. We should organize a boycott."

"MIT is already boycotting me, Sara."

"Whatever. They suck." She steps back, her hands on my arms. "Let me look at you. Oh ma gah! You got your contacts!"

"Keep it down. People are staring."

She covers her mouth briefly. "You look amazing! How are they?"

"Except for the pain, I love them." I pull the bottle of eye-lube out of my purse, tilt my head back, and squeeze a few drops into each eye. "My eyes are a little dry." When I blink, the fake tears run down my cheek, making a mess.

Sara digs out a tissue and hands it to me. "Have you figured out which safety you're going to accept?"

"Um, I actually have a Plan B." I wipe my face clean. "I'm going to appeal. I think maybe . . . maybe they made a mistake."

While I explain my plan to ambush MIT, Teri Litch wanders briefly into sight. Her cart contains three economy-sized jugs of grape juice, a huge box of oatmeal, two cases of soda, and countless bags of potato chips and pretzels. She carefully looks over the raspberries and boysenberries, the most expensive fruit in the store, and picks out two boxes of each.

Sara frowns. "This might work. You'll need a different car, though. And you have to weasel your way into the admissions office."

"Yeah, I know."

"What does your dad think?"

"He's been too busy to talk about it."

"I guess that's typical, huh? Tell you what, we can work on your plan instead of going to the movies."

"Since when are we going to the movies?"

"I forgot to tell you." She grins and waggles her eyebrows. "We were going to kidnap you: me, Travis, and Mitch. That's why I'm here."

"Isn't kidnapping illegal?"

"Not when you do it to save your best friend from certain despair. You wouldn't answer any of our calls or e-mail. We were afraid you were freaking out, like go-on-medication, get-a-shrink, seriously freaking out. We were going to force you to sit through a vampire movie and eat cheese fries."

"I hate cheese fries."

"Cheese fries are good for the soul. But that's beside the point. We don't need the cheese fries therapy because you're here, you're talking to me, you're okay."

"Not so fast," I say.

She zooms in close. "Now what?"

"Teri Litch is living in my bedroom."

"No way."

"Big way." Teri passes by the end of the aisle again while I give Sara the gory details. Sara's eyes are huge. "So she could be living with you until graduation?"

"She could be living with me all summer."

"You seriously need cheese fries."

"Thank you, I think. Look, there's Travis."

Travis bursts through the swinging doors carrying a box of apples. Only Travis Baird could make a Superfresh uniform look cool. The skull-and-crossbones sticker on his nametag is an elegant touch.

"Babe," he says, setting the apples on the floor.

"Sweetie." Sara glides toward him. They embrace and suck face in the French tradition. The ice under the pomegranates melts. I'm definitely buying them a carton of condoms for graduation.

The doors swing open again and out pops a short, middle-aged guy in an uncool Superfresh uniform. He has gold stars on his nametag (Manager Ed) and is pushing a cart loaded with bleach. Travis peels himself off Sara and whispers something in her ear. She saunters back to me, hot-eyed and hungry.

"He's going to meet me in the bakery," she says.

"All that sugar," I say.

"And frosting. He gets off in twenty minutes. We'll go to the diner and plan your road trip to MIT."

"I don't know, Sar, I've got Teri with me and—"

"Twenty minutes. And keep your eyes open for Mitch. He should be here soon."


After she leaves, I wander the aisles and pick up a bag of Chee·tos and some soap. I love Chee·tos. I love orange Chee·tos dust under my fingernails. Since I'm indulging myself, I decide to buy a box of ice cream sandwiches, too. I'll wait until everybody goes to bed and eat them all by myself.

Mitchell Pangborn tracks me down in frozen foods.

"Hey," he says. "I saw your car in the parking lot."

"Hey."

I look him over carefully, using my contact-enhanced laser vision. He's wearing a sweat-soaked T-shirt from Pangborn Landscaping, filthy jeans, and boots. His arms are scratched, his face a little sunburned. God, he's hot.

"I thought Sara said we were going to take you to the movies."

"I ruined the plans. Is this how you dress for a kidnapping?"

He looks down and brushes the mulch from the front of his shirt. "Dad made me work until it got dark, then I had to unload the trucks. I came straight here. I've been worried about you, Malone, really worried."

An old man says, "Excuse me," and reaches in front of Mitch to open a freezer door. We stand quietly as he stares at the selection of Hearty Man meals. He chooses Hearty Beef Stew, closes the door, and shuffles away. Ice crystals hang in the air.

Mitch steps closer and puts his hands on the end of my cart. The metal conducts an electric current from his body to mine. It makes my fingertips tingle.

"I was worried," he says again.

"I didn't want to talk to anyone."

"Not even me?"

There are many fine things about Mitchell Pangborn's body, but his hands are near the top of the list. My magic contacts let me examine every detail: the calluses, the mulch under his nails, the tendons and veins, the soft part at the base of his thumb. I want to touch them. I want them to touch me, to thaw me, bring me up to room temperature. Mitchell Pangborn's thumbs running down the length of my spine. His hands on my—

"What are you going to do, Kate? I mean really, all bull-shit aside, what are you going to do?"

The tone of his voice snaps me out of the fantasy. I blink. "Appeal. I think they made a mistake."

"That's crap."

"No, it's not. I think the computer screwed up."

He makes a face. "It's crap and you know it. You didn't get in, babe. You have to deal with it."

Red warning lights flash behind my contacts. "That's a little harsh, don't you think?"

"It's not harsh, it's real." He takes his hands off the cart and lowers his voice. "Deluding yourself won't help anything, Malone."

"Excuse me? You're in Harvard, you've known for months. You don't know what this feels like."

He puts his hands on his hips. More mulch flakes fall to the floor. "It's not that difficult to figure out. Lots of people don't get into their top school, and you know I'm sorry that you didn't, but it's not the end of the world. Choose one of your safeties and send in your deposit. End of story."

This is why we need to do more kissing and less talking. I push the cart back and forth a few inches. I wonder if Mikey likes ice cream sandwiches. Maybe I should get Popsicles instead. Less mess.

"I'll come over tomorrow after church," he says. "I'll help you choose."

"No."

"What?"

"I don't need your help. Besides, I'll be busy tomorrow. The Litches have moved in with us. Did you know that? Teri's little brother is adorable. I have to get him some Popsicles. I'll see you on Monday."

As I swing the cart around him, he grabs it again.

"What the hell is going on? You aren't you."

I can't move the cart.

"Are you high? Is it lack of sleep? You're scaring me, Kate."

I take a deep breath, fortify my shields, strengthen the force field. "I'm busy and I'm tired, and I want you to let go of my cart. I am going to talk to the admissions department at MIT. If for some ungodly reason they really don't want me, then—and only then—will I look at other schools."

"Look at other schools?"

"Pick one of the safeties."

He won't release the cart. "You did apply to other schools, right? You never got around to showing me those essays."

"What do you think I am, nuts? Of course I did." I yank the cart out of his hands and walk toward the front of the store. The wheels are out of alignment; the cart wants to veer right and crash into the shelves.

"Come back, Kate."

"I'll see you Monday," I say over my shoulder.

Teri is nowhere to be seen. Neither is Sara, or Travis. I wrestle the cart into the express aisle and pay for my Chee·tos and soap. I'll buy Popsicles at 7-Eleven. I want out of here, now.

Somebody in the parking lot leans on a horn. It doesn't blare, it bleats like a sick goat. That's Bert's horn.

I look through the plateglass window. Teri has Bert parked, engine idling, right in front of the window. She's in the driver's seat. She waves her hand, motioning for me to join her.

I run outside. "What the hell are you doing? How did you get this started?"

Teri leans over and opens the passenger door. "Get in," she says. "I think they called the cops on me."

## 4.4 ▌ Activation Energy

I jump in the car, slam the door, and grab the dashboard as Teri floors it. She squeals the tires as we leave the parking lot. The good news is that this car is barely capable of making the speed limit, much less breaking it, so we won't be pulled over for going too fast. The bad news? Teri is driving.

We turn right, we turn left, we double back, we turn left, she pulls a U-turn and burns rubber again. My stomach flips and I have a nasty flashback to fifth grade when Dad took Toby and me on the Mad Hatter's Teacups at Disney World and I upchucked cotton candy everywhere.

"You'd better slow down," I say. "No, just stop. Stop. The engine is going to overheat and I can't afford a new one."

Teri pulls into the mall parking lot and cruises to a spot in the shadows behind Sears. I wipe my palms on my pants. She chuckles and pulls a pack of cigarettes and a lighter from her shirt pocket.

"You think this is funny?" I ask.

"Yep." She shakes out a cigarette and lights it. "I thought you were going to shit your pants. Don't worry. Nobody's coming after us."

I listen. No sirens. "What do you mean?"

She inhales, and the glowing end of the cigarette reflects off her glasses. She blows the smoke to my side of the car.

I wave the smoke away and roll down the window. "Did they call the police or not?"

She shrugs. "They might have."

"Might have?"

She shrugs again.

I take off my seat belt and check the back. It's empty. "What happened to the food in your cart?"

She slips the lighter into the cellophane sleeve of the cigarette pack and puts it back in her pocket. "I hid it in the bushes behind the loading dock. We can pick it up later."

"No, we can't."

"Why not?"

"I don't steal food. Or cars."

"I didn't steal your car. You're sitting right here."

"How did you get it started?"

"I hot-wired it. Piece of cake. Want me to teach you how?"

"No, thank you. I'll use my keys."

Teri takes another drag and sucks the smoke deep into her lungs. "Suit yourself."

Bert's engine ticks loudly as it cools. I stare through the windshield at the brick wall in front of us. "So you were stealing, but you didn't get caught, but you pretended the cops were coming. Why?"

Teri blows a smoke ring that loops around the rearview mirror. "That geek. You've been ducking his phone calls, right? I thought maybe he was dogging you. I was trying to help. Don't thank me or nothing."

"Thank you? I should thank you?"

"Yeah, I think so."

She pulls out the ashtray, but it's full of lavender potpourri. She flicks the cigarette ash on her jeans and rubs in it with the palm of her hand. Smoke hangs around her head like a dirty veil. It is so quiet I can hear the water leaking from the radiator.

I clear my throat. "All right. You were trying to be nice. Thank you. But I don't need help."

"Suit yourself." She rubs more ashes on her jeans.

"I'm just having a hard time right now," I say.

"That's right, I forgot. No college for Katie. And I have no idea what it's like, right?"

"That's not what I mean."

"Right." She takes a drag and blows smoke at the ceiling.

"I need you to smoke outside. I can't stand it."

"It's too cold. Don't be such a bitch."

"Me? A bitch?"

"Yeah, you're a major bitch."

"I'm letting you sleep in *my* room, live in *my* house."

"Your dad is making you do that. If it was up to you, I'd be on the street."

I stare at the wall again.

Teri rolls down her window and the trapped smoke escapes. Noise from the boulevard filters in with the cold air; cars shifting gears, accelerating, braking.

"Let me ask you a question," she says.

I grit my teeth. "Go ahead."

"Your dad. Is he for real, offering to help us out?"

"What do you mean?"

"I'm speaking English, right? He said the church will fix our house for free. What's in it for him?"

"It makes him happy. It makes him look good."

"He won't go to court to get the house or nothing?"

I turn and look at her. "No. He would never try that. He just wants to do the right thing. It's his job."

"Hmm."

Bert's temperature gauge has inched out of the danger zone. I'll give it another minute, just to be safe. I study the pattern of the bricks in front of us. Somewhere in the warped recesses of my brain, an idea ignites.

"How much do you know about building houses?" I ask.

"Lots. I took all the courses at the vo-tech, worked construction last summer." Teri picks at the MIT sticker on the dash with her thumbnail. "Why?"

"I bet they'd listen to you, if you told them what you wanted done. You could be in control, or help at least. I bet it would get done faster, too, if you were supervising things."

Her nail slides under a corner of the sticker. "Probably."

"Let's face it. Neither one of us is happy with the living arrangements right now."

"Got that right. Your house is a damn psycho ward. And the phone never stops ringing."

"So I'll convince Dad that you should be allowed to help rebuild your own house. The sooner it's done, the sooner we can both go back to normal life."

She smoothes the corner of the sticker back in place. "Suits me fine. "

"Me, too." I unbuckle my seat belt. "We have a deal. Switch seats with me, I'm driving."

# 5.0 | Alchemy

*SAFETY TIP: Open reagent packages only after reading and understanding label.*

Church looks way different with my contacts in. For one thing, I can see what everyone is praying for. My father up there is praying for enough people to help out at the Litches, and for the suppliers to cut him a fifty percent break on the materials. Betty, sitting at the organ, is praying that she remembered to turn the iron off at home. Toby, next to me, is praying for X-rated things that should get him struck by lightning. Mikey, sitting on the floor in front of Mrs. Litch, is playing, not praying.

I fight to keep my eyes open. Mikey snored again last night, so I put on my sneakers and ran until I got lost, then I kept running. It was like I had an extra lung or something. The farther I ran, the more energy I had. And then I came home and watched television until Mikey woke up.

Construction noise echoes off the hills and penetrates the stained-glass windows. If I listen hard enough, I can hear the sound of the rotten parts of Teri's house being ripped up. Not all the volunteers go to our church, and some of them have been working since breakfast. Teri went down there with a flashlight before the sun rose.

I pray to Zeus. To Hera. To Thor, Loki, Freya, Aphrodite, to Jesus, to Mohammed, to Moses, to Lord Vishnu and Ganesha and the Turtle with the World on His Back and to the Godplace I lost in me when I wasn't looking: Let me in. Let me in MIT. You all know I belong there, I need to be there, it's all I've ever wanted, it's what I've worked for my entire life. Let me in and I'll be nice to Teri, honestly, truly nice. I'll live up to every standard of charity and kindness. I'll help her with her house, her brother, her mom, her hair. I'll find her a date. I'll find her a job. I know you're testing me. I'm good at tests.

After I murmur "Amen," it occurs to me that I don't pray. Too late.

The congregation stands to sing. Toby is glued to the Game Boy hidden in his hymnal. When we sit back down, Mikey crawls into my lap. Two minutes into Dad's sermon, the kid is sound asleep—not snoring. I smooth his hair and press his head against my shoulder. I wish my contacts could see into his head, see the world through his eyes. What would he think of MIT? Of college? All he cares about are trucks and cartoons and cereal. And Teri; he worships her.

Dad's sermon wanders through the Old Testament, skims across the New Testament, touches down by Walden Pond, and borrows the wisdom of Woody Guthrie and Nelson Mandela to make his point about helping neighbors and building community. If I were feeling cynical, I'd point out that he is guilting the congregation into helping the Litches. But he's so happy, so earnestly, ministerly, Dadly happy; this is what he was put on earth to do, to remind people how to be nice to one another.

Mikey stirs, turns his face. The cheek that was lying against me is damp with sweat. I blow gently on his skin to cool it down. I wish there were someone big enough to hold me in their lap so I could nap. No, a coma. I wish I could slip into a coma for a few months. That would feel good.

I just need a way to get through this week. I have to find a way to get some sleep, deal with MIT, put up with all the withering, pitying, gloating looks from my classmates, evade the well-meaning support of teachers, not piss off Teri, figure out why Mitch is beginning to bug me, and stop running. I think I can do it.

Please, gods.

# 6.0 | Electrostatic Forces

*SAFETY TIP: Use gloves when handling steel wool.*

By Monday morning, Operation Amish Rebuild is in full swing. Teri blows off school so she can work with Pete and his construction crew. My job is to drive Mikey to preschool, the one at Merryweather High. It feels weird, looking in the rearview mirror and seeing him waving at me. I sing the elements song fifty million times. He says "Twuck."

Cerberus the security guard stops us at the door to school. I have my ID card out and ready.

"Do you want to see his, too?" I ask.

Her upper lip twitches. "Why do you have Teri Litch's little brother with you?"

"He's an extra-credit project."

"Don't get an attitude with me, missy."

I consider biting off her head, but it would set a bad example. I do the boring thing and explain about Teri, house, fire, yadda-yadda. She waves us through. Once we are through the lobby, I swear under my breath. Mikey repeats what I say, as loud as humanly possible.

"I heard that!" bellows the security guard.

"We definitely need to work on your vocab, pal," I tell him.

As we walk past the *Student Body* sculpture, Mikey growls like a bear, then bursts out laughing.

After I drop off Mikey, I have to face my failure and humiliation. Chem class is torture. People keep looking at me with pity and Diana won't let me touch the Bunsen burner. The guidance office is still jammed with bodies.

Mitch isn't in the cafeteria second period and that's just fine with me. I do not want to finish the conversation he started in the grocery store. Sara makes me eat a jelly doughnut and then forces me to write up a list of options. She wants me to "free my imagination, be bold." Here is what I come up with:

**Quantum Futures**

1. Get MIT to admit they made a mistake. Enroll.
2. Sue MIT to get them to admit they made a mistake. Enroll.
3. Steal identity from someone who was mistakenly let in. No, can't do that.
4. I still like Option #1.
5. (Okay, Sara. How's this?) Apply to Stanford.
6. Drive to MIT and force them to admit they made a mistake. Enroll.

I don't say anything to Mitch in English. Things feel wicked out of sync with him.

I gut out the stares and gleeful whispers that follow me all day. Everybody loves a loser. Coach Reid won't let me practice because of the Treadmill Incident on Friday. I try to explain, but he orders me to take three days off. It's a conspiracy, I swear.

One day, over. Whew.

## 6.1 ▍ Atomic Structure

After school, I take Mikey to see the progress on his house. Teri meets us on the side porch, wearing dirty work clothes, a leather tool belt, and a hint of a smile.

"Was he good today?" she asks.

Mikey leans out of my arms and into hers. She settles him on her hip, above her belt.

"He was great," I say. "He waved to every truck driver on the way to school and back."

I step back so two burly guys can carry a charred mattress out the door. The house is filled with the sounds of saws, hammers, and high-powered fans. It still smells of bitter smoke.

"Can I have a tour?" I ask.

"Suit yourself. Not much to see yet, but it'll get there."

She steps inside and I follow. The curtains have been

taken off the living room windows and all the furniture stacked in the middle. As we cross the room, the carpet squishes under our feet. The fire didn't get this far, but the water from the fire hoses did.

"Yeah, it's a mess, I know," Teri says. "You've got to use your imagination." She taps bare wood at the far end of the room, where the carpet has been pulled back. "We're going to sand this. Coat it good with polyurethane."

"It'll look nice."

"Yeah. I like hardwood floors." She hikes Mikey higher on her hip, walks across the hall, and opens a door. The windows in here are covered with blankets, and a table in the center of the room is piled high with boxes. "This used to be the dining room, before Charlie's junk took it over. I want to make it into a playroom. There's hardwood under that rug, too. We could use new baseboards and crown molding, but they're luxuries at this point."

"Who's Charlie?"

Mikey pops his thumb in his mouth and sucks hard.

"He was our father," Teri says, closing the door.

She's on the move again, down the hall to the back of the house. "The kitchen is a wreck, but it was a wreck before the fire, so no loss there."

I look over her shoulder. The work crew has already finished what the fire had started; the kitchen has been completely gutted, stripped down to the beams under the floor. Mikey's thumb slips out of his mouth at the sight.

"We're almost ready to lay a new subfloor," Teri says.

"That'll go fast. What I really want to do is to frame out the wall so we can bust through an opening into the playroom, see, have it be one big open area. We could work around the load-bearing beams, that's not a problem."

"I have no idea what you're talking about."

"That's why you're not in charge here. The problem is convincing Pete that it's worth the time to frame out the opening. He's a real moron. "

"If you say so."

She walks back down the hall. "We're leaving the bathroom alone for now, though someday I'd like to do some tile work in there." Teri shifts Mikey to her other hip. "Most of the first floor is cosmetic, except for the kitchen. Upstairs is going to take a little longer. Watch your step."

We climb over the child safety gate at the foot of the stairs and head up. Mikey puts his arms around her neck. Halfway up the stairs, the banister stops. The higher we climb, the heavier the smell of smoke. The work crew crawling around on the roof sounds like they're about to fall through on top of us. I stick close to the wall. "I thought the fire only affected the roof."

"It burned through in a couple of places, and there's a lot of water damage." Teri waits for me at the top of the stairs. "We have some old Charlie damage, too."

"What is Charlie damage?"

Mikey squirms in his sister's arms, and Teri slides him around her body so that he's riding piggyback. "Charlie rewired the house and ran an illegal tap off the power lines out front. Cheap SOB. The code officer freaked when he saw it. He won't let us move back in until everything is up to code. Guess how long it will take."

"Months?"

She chuckles. "Nah. Couple of weeks, tops. Don't be so gullible. Your dad found a guy who said he'd do it and only charge for parts. Come on, I'll show you Mikey's room."

The doors along the dark hall are all closed. One has three locks installed in a column above the doorknob, like a television version of a New York City apartment.

"Who do you have locked up in there?"

Teri reaches down and jingles her key ring. "That's my room. And no, I'm not showing you. Here." She opens the door at the end of the hall.

Mikey's bedroom is small, with tall dormer windows on three sides. One window looks straight up the hill to our house. The walls and ceiling are smoke stained. Some furniture is stacked in a corner: a crib, a chair, dented cardboard boxes of toys and clothes. Mikey squirms to get down and play, but Teri locks her arms under his legs. The electrical outlets have been pulled from the walls, and their wires writhe and coil.

"I know exactly what I want this to look like," she says. "I want to put wainscoting on the bottom third of the wall and build in a chalkboard so he'll have a place to draw. I want built-in shelves where he can keep his toys and books and stuff. And a big-boy bed. If we run out of money, I could probably make one from scrap lumber."

"I'm sure someone will find him a bed," I say.

"When he gets older, we'll get him a desk. A computer, too."

"Ucky," Mikey says, still squirming to break free.

"No way, dude," Teri says. She spins in a tight circle. "You're not getting down." She spins faster to distract him. Mikey giggles and throws his head back. Teri whirls like a centrifuge, her boots thudding the floor until she stumbles a bit, slows down, and stops. Mikey rests his face between her shoulder blades, still giggling.

"So." Teri hikes up her tool belt. "Feel like helping?" she asks.

"I'd, um, I'd love to, but I don't know how to do any of this."

"Let's see if you can learn how to hold a hammer."

Of course I can hold a hammer. Any idiot can hold a hammer. It's the *act* of hammering, the physics of the process, that I'm struggling with. I've never been completely comfortable with physics.

"No, no, no," Teri says for the eighty-third time. "Like this."

She holds a nail with her left hand (no, I will not comment on her black thumbnail, I will not, I will not, I will not), takes a breath, and *bam*—*bam*—BAM! The nail slides into the wood like butter. She's doing the real thing, nailing the kitchen subflooring to whatever they're called, the long boards under the floor. She pulls a nail from the pouch on her tool belt, sets it, *bam—bam*—BAM!

"Isn't there something called a nail gun?" I ask. "Wouldn't that be easier?"

"This is a low-budget job," Teri says. "We're powered by muscle and sweat, the old-fashioned way. Try again."

I take a breath. Weight, velocity, and angle. Remember to hit the nail in the center of the head. *Tap—tap*—damn! The nail droops sadly to one side. I killed it, just like I killed all the other bent nails in my little test board.

"I don't know, Kate. Maybe you're not made for real work. You should stick to school."

"Cut me some slack. I've never done this before." *Bam—bam—thonk.* "Damn."

Teri pries the bent nail out of the wood and throws it to the ground. "Kate Malone, you suck at hammering."

I drop the hammer in the dirt. "Is there something else I can do? Sawing, maybe."

"You'd be dangerous around a saw. Have you always been a spaz?"

"I'm not answering that."


I wait until everyone goes to sleep, then I put on my sneakers and head outside. The houses that line the streets are the walls of a maze I'm trying to find my way out of. My breath feels as if it's coming from a different body. I am afraid to open my mouth and talk to myself because there is a chance I might start to scream. It's like I've been chopped into tiny pieces of Kate, and all my pieces look like me and run like me and talk like me and act just the right way, but they are all lost in this maze. Bad Kate (still stalking me) says the maze has always been there, I'm just seeing it for the first time because of these contacts. Good Kate says nonsense, it's time to go to bed.

## 6.2 ▌ Experimentation

Breakfast with the Litch siblings is loud. Mikey spills grape juice twice and Teri burns the oatmeal. She's pumped about her house, though. Keeps talking about Palladian windows. (I've got to look that word up when she's not around.) Dad tries to get parental about how she should be in school and work on the house on the weekends. I suggest that we talk to the vo-tech supervisor, see if Teri can get credit for what she's doing. Dad scowls and Mikey spills his grape juice again.

Mikey gets through the security at school without causing a scene. He has not blown out a diaper for forty-eight hours. Progress.

Mr. Kennedy, my guidance counselor, finally sees me fourth period on Tuesday. He tells me my options, the not-quantum ones. Basically, I'm screwed. My father can call MIT to make sure they rejected the right person, but there is no way they'll reconsider my application. He says if I really don't want to attend any of the schools that "accepted" me (let's hope it's not a sin to lie to your guidance counselor), I can apply to a school with rolling admissions, and hope to transfer to MIT after a year. Or I can I take a year off to "get my act together." How sixties of him. I leave his office with a stack of brochures that I will give to Mikey to destroy.

When I get home, everybody is down at the Litches'. Teri and Pete are feuding about opening the wall between the kitchen and playroom. Since she's busy, I put myself in charge of asset management. I am Queen of Lists and I make Mikey my Prince. He and I walk around the house, writing up highly technical documents like this:

**A Litch List: Restoration Requirements, p. 1**
3 fans from fire company
80 gallons white paint
10 gallons colored paint (Betty said Jesus told her the
     place needs accent colors)
paintbrushes
3 gallons window cleaner
18 rolls paper towels
13 kitchen ladies, armed with brooms and scrub brushes
     and Mr. Clean
4 mousetraps
cheese
assorted sledgehammers and crowbars
work gloves for everybody
kitchen cabinets
roofing materials
refrigerator

stove

sink

1 gigantic Dumpster

industrial sander for big things

100 pieces of sandpaper for little things

countless pieces of wood

nails for wood

hammers for nails

Mikey draws cows on the other side of the paper. They look like deflated balloons, but I know they are cows.

I corner Dad before dinner, when Teri is in the shower and Toby is teaching Mikey a video game. He flat out refuses to help me with the MIT appeal. He won't even consider asking the admissions office why they turned me down, because he thinks I'm being slightly deranged about the topic. As for me driving to Cambridge to talk to the admissions officer face-to-face, well, his response makes it clear he's been spending way too much time around the Litch family. If Betty heard him use language like that, she'd tell Jesus, for sure.

## 6.3 ▍ Hydrochloric

It's hard to keep the days straight because whoever is running my life has pointed the Giant Remote at me and pushed

Pause. Days just ooze by randomly, one after another.

Breakfast *chez* Malone provides our recommended daily requirement of chaos: lost homework, dirty diapers, forgotten phone messages, crumpled construction estimates, tools on the counter, juice spilled in the refrigerator, broken toys, a tsunami of laundry, chewed crayons, abandoned books, and oatmeal. There is peace in my car, just me and Mikey and the miles to school. We practice singing the elements song and the alphabet, and counting. This kid is a lot smarter than Teri realizes. He can say "Kate" and "Spock" and "atom." I spend my second period lunches in his preschool class. We build towers.

Classwork and homework are produced by the Kate-a-tron, operating at a tolerable performance level. Everything is under control, with the possible exception of Mitchell "Why Won't You Answer My Calls?" Pangborn. Sara understands how busy I am with the Litch Invasion. Travis understands. My father and brother get it. Even the dog is giving me some extra space.

By the end of the week I have a few things to add to the Quantum Futures List:

7. Become an Olympic runner.
8. Become a leading childcare expert.
9. Become a construction consultant.
10. Create a new career: Chaos Manager.
11. Rehabilitate the title: Domestic Goddess.

12. Make a movie about why MIT should let me in. Enroll.
13. Reapply to MIT. Pay someone to write my essays. Enroll.
14. Take a year off and chill (as if).

The lines between my days and my nights are blurring. The night is filled with the calls of owls and the smell of daffodils, and I run for miles.

# 7.0 | Nuclear Stability

*SAFETY TIP: Develop an accident plan.*

I work at the pharmacy until three o'clock on Saturday, then I change into cruddy clothes and hurry down the hill. Dad had more than forty people volunteer to work today, and they had great weather. I can't wait to see how much they got done.

(40 people + good weather) x motivation = a miracle.

Incredible. All that is left of the barn is a neatly raked rectangle bordered by foundation stones. The roof of the house is patched, the gutters have been fixed, and the shutters all taken down. Every window is open to catch the breeze. The kitchen has walls and a roof, a door, and a bay window that looks out over the pond. The air is filled with the sounds of hammers, saws, and some kind of buzzing noise I don't recognize. When it dies down, I can hear a radio playing and people laughing, shouting, talking. The smell of smoke has been replaced by the smell of new lumber, varnish, and paint: hopeful smells.

I walk up onto the porch and step inside. The living room is unrecognizable. Everything, absolutely every stick of furniture, has been removed and the rug torn out. The hard-wood floor glows. I move down the hall. The kitchen is busy with one guy installing a sink while his buddy sticks tiles in place on the wall where the stove will go. A third guy is sweeping up sawdust. The appliances aren't in yet, but the cabinets are all hung. Amazing.

The playroom is where the buzzing noise was coming from. A woman with a mask over her mouth is pushing a giant sander over the floor. Two other women wait until she turns it off, then they follow and clean up behind her. The windows are still grimy, but the floor is looking pretty good. Cans of paint are stacked in the corner, along with floor cloths, brushes, and wooden paint stirrers.

With the sander off again, I can hear all kinds of commotion upstairs, including Teri's voice telling somebody that "a blind man could see that thing isn't straight." If she doesn't lighten up with these guys, they're going to quit. Teri and I need to have a chat about the concept of team play.

I walk back down the hall, past the parlor, where three guys are busy painting the walls a soft shade of pink. I step through the front door (new doorknob) to the front yard, where the command post has been set up. Betty and Mrs. Litch are crocheting under the new shade of the maple tree. This is the first time I've seen Mrs. Litch here since the fire. Mikey is playing with his trucks on the ground in front of them. I don't have the nerve to ask what they are crocheting. It's big and orange; could be a car cover, maybe a fishing net.

Mr. Lockheart is scraping paint off the shutters while Dad

watches him intensely. Mr. Lockheart knows better than to let my father touch any tools. Dad's job is to look encouraging and to hum; he's very good at humming. He carries things, too. He's not a big guy, but he's sturdy, and whenever something heavy needs to be moved, they call for the Reverend.

Ms. Cummings is pinning wet curtains to a clothesline strung from the maple tree to the front of the house. Toby is washing windows. The kitchen ladies are scrubbing inside. The choir is scraping old paint off the shutters. Everybody has a job. Hammer. Measure. Saw. Sweep. Scrub. Sand. Paint. Boss around. Play with trucks in the grass. Crochet. Gossip.

Mikey is the first one to notice me. "'Mony, Kate."

"Antimony to you, too, Mikey." What a kid.

Betty looks up from her crocheting. "There you are, dear. We were just talking about you."

I force a smile. "Of course you were. Um, is there anything I can do to help?"

"You missed another spot," Toby says.

I spray the window cleaner directly in his face. It's a shame we are separated by a pane of dirty glass. My brother is a tyrant. This is the seventh window we have washed together. For a slob, he is strangely concerned about clean glass. It's taking fifteen minutes to do each one. If he keeps this up, he won't live to see number eight.

"No, you didn't get it yet." Toby frowns. "Right there. Rub harder."

"If I rub any harder the glass is going to break."

"Wuss."

I rub so hard that paint chips flake off the frame and float to the ground. "Better?"

"A little."

He moves down to the next window and sprays. It takes me longer. I have to climb down the ladder, move the ladder, check and make sure the ladder is properly positioned, ascend halfway, scoot back down, make a few more safety adjustments, then climb up the seven rungs to the top.

"Could you be any slower?" asks my always-supportive sibling.

"You missed a spot," I say.

He coughs once and coats the glass with spray cleaner. It looks like a wave hit it. I concentrate on my side. After a while I don't notice Toby's face or his hands on the other side. We work in silence until the pane is so clear you can't see anything between us.

"Looks good," I say. "Open up."

He hits the frame, struggles, then slides the window open six inches.

"Last one on this floor," he says. "We'll have to get the big ladder for the upstairs."

My toes try to curl around the rung I am standing on. "It's getting too late. You have to wash windows when the sun is high enough to see the streaks."

"Whatever. We could do it tomorrow after church, I guess." He sits down on the floor so that his chin is even with the windowsill.

"You like doing this?"

"Yeah. It's kind of fun. Spooky, but fun."

"Spooky how?"

"They carted out hundreds of beer bottles and a bunch of guns this morning. I heard Pete say some of the walls upstairs have holes in them. Don't you think that's spooky— living in a house that has holes in the walls?"

I use a paper towel to brush away the loose paint chips and dead flies from the windowsill. "Yeah. But all that stuff was from Teri's dad and he's dead. Good-bye, scumbag."

"I guess." He spies a smudge on the glass, sprays it, and wipes carefully. "But here's what I don't get. Why didn't they do any of this cleaning or repair work before? Dad said Mr. Litch died last year."

"He died in jail," I remind him.

"Whatever. He was dead. He couldn't come back and put more holes in the wall. Why didn't they fix it up themselves?"

I peel off more flakes of paint with my fingernail. Little worms are chewing their way through the wood. "No money, no time, no energy. Remind me to show this to Teri. I bet all the frames are rotting. They'll have to be replaced."

"Maybe that's another reason. Once you get started on something like this, it just gets bigger and bigger." He stops to cough. It's amazing he lasted this long with all the sawdust, paint fumes, and mold spores floating around.

"You're done, Tobe. Time for some clean air. Out of there."

"Give me a break."

"Seriously. I shouldn't have let you stay in there so long. You want to use the nebulizer?"

"Quit babying me." *Cough.* "I'm fine." *Cough, hack, wheeze.*

"Pizza!" someone calls from the front of the house.

"Yes!" Toby bolts in the direction of the food, hacking all the way.

I descend the ladder slowly, feeling with my toes to find the ground.


## 7.1 ▌Synthesis

Mitchell A. Pangborn's Saturn has become the pizza delivery van. He parks it and unloads the boxes from the trunk, handing them to Travis and Sara, who carry them to the side porch. I think I want to say hi to him, but I have to wash my hands first.

Ms. Cummings and Mikey walk down the hill bearing leftover tuna casserole. Some volunteers use the arrival of dinner as their cue to head home, but a good dozen stay to chow down.

Before the pizza is dished out, Dad asks us all hold hands and bow our heads for grace. Mikey drags Teri over to me so he can stand between us. When we take his hands, he pulls his feet up off the ground and swings back and forth, his eyes squeezed shut. Dad blesses the house, the food, the families and friends gathered around the pizza boxes. Then he grins and blesses the pepperoni, sausage, green peppers, onions, and extra cheese.

"Amen. Dig in."

Teri carries a plate to her mother, sitting in the best folding chair on the porch, then she sits down beside her to wolf down a slice of pepperoni. Teri's face has gotten tanned this week, and I swear her biceps are even bigger.

Mikey is wired. He climbs into Mrs. Litch's lap and eats a few bites of her pizza, then slides to the floor and rolls his toy fire truck around, scooting the length of the porch on his knees. When he gets to me, he drives the truck up my back and into my hair. I pretend to growl. He giggles and crawls away.

Travis takes his boom box out of Mitch's car and turns it on. My father listens to the mildly obscene hip-hop for a minute, then fiddles with the dial until he finds a jazz station. Mrs. Litch unexpectedly pipes up and tells us about going to a jazz festival in Central Park in New York City when she was fifteen, "before I met Charlie, of course." She says that when she squeezed her eyes, she could see the notes like colors splashing in front of her.

It is hard to imagine Mrs. Litch was ever fifteen years old.

Mikey steals a few noodles from the casserole dish, stuffs them in his mouth, and runs inside.

"Is everything cleaned up in there?" Teri asks.

"He's fine. All the tools are put away," Dad says. "I closed the paint cans myself. The place is as clean as a whistle."

I stretch across Sara's legs and take another slice of extra cheese and onion. The conversation drifts back to jazz, to paint colors, to the sunset. After a few minutes, Mikey comes back out, his hands covered with thick yellow paint.

"Ucky," he says.

Everybody breaks up in laughter.

"What? What's that?" Mrs. Litch asks, squinting. "What happened?"

Teri picks up her brother. "Picasso here was decorating, Ma. I'll clean him up."

As she washes him off in the downstairs bathroom, Mikey babbles about his big trucks and his big-boy room. "Big boy" is the phrase of the day. Through the window, I can see Teri close and lock the door to the future playroom, where the paint cans are. She puts Mikey down to play with his trucks on the smooth living room floor and comes back out, sits next to me, and steals my pizza crust.

I lean my head against the side of the house. We're done for the night. Everyone is beat, happy and beat. The old people talk about jazz some more, trumpets, saxophones, drums. Mitchell collects the dirty plates and napkins and puts them in a trash bag, then he sits down on the other side of me. He showered just before he picked up the pizza. I can smell the soap on his neck. I am too tired to move away, almost too tired to be irritated at him anymore. I'm just going to pretend that a very good-smelling, incredibly warm stranger is sitting next to me, a harmless stranger.

The sun is setting. A few months ago, it would have been dark by now. Mr. Lockheart flicks a switch and the feeble porch light flickers on. A moth bangs into the dirty glass. We should put that on the to-do list: clean porch light.

My dad tells a dumb joke and Mrs. Litch laughs. Mitchell chuckles. I am on the edge of dropping off; I could actually fall asleep here. Someone else tells a joke. People laugh harder and I open my eyes. The porch light goes out, fades away without a flicker. It must have been an old bulb. The confused moth flutters away.

"Did you hear that?" Teri asks.

"It's crickets, Theresa," Mrs. Litch says. "Spring is here to stay."

"I think the power went out," Dad says.

Teri twists around and looks through the open door to the living room. She stands and walks down the steps, peers at the side yard, then jogs around the house. I stand up and look through the door. The living room is empty.

Mr. Lockheart frowns. "Power can't be out." He pulls a flashlight from his belt and turns it on. "Of course, if something caused a short, a mouse or—"

"Mikey's gone." Teri leaps up the porch steps and runs in the house. "Mikey! Mii-key!" She thuds through the house like a giant, the floors shaking under the urgent weight of her boots.

"He's probably in front of the television," says Mrs. Litch.

"They packed the television away, dear," Betty says quietly.

"Mii-keeey!"

The air crackles.

"I'll check the road," Sara says.

"The pond," Mitch says. He jumps off the porch and sprints to the backyard.

I follow Teri into the house. "Mikey? Mikey?"

"MIIIIII-KEEEEEEYYYY!" bellows Teri.

I meet her at the foot of the stairs.

The safety gate has been ripped down.

Teri bolts up the stairs, fear trailing her like thunder.

# 0.0.0 | Quantum Shift

Mikey lies in his room, in his big-boy room. He lies on the bare floor. He lies on the bare floor, his fingertips stretched to the snakes in the electrical outlet. His red fire truck, the one with the metal ladder that moves up and down, is blackened. The wall around the electrical outlet is charred. As I watch, a wisp of smoke escapes out the open window.

Time screeches to a halt, reeking of burnt rubber.

Outside someone turns down the radio, draining away Mrs. Litch's jazz. I can hear doors closing, the sound of someone running.

"It doesn't look like he's been near the pond," Travis tells my father.

"None of the weeds have been stepped on. He's not there," says Mitch.

They sound like men, grown men far away at the other end of a metal tube.

Mikey Litch lies on the bare floor of his big-boy room, his eyes open and empty.

Children don't die. Not really, not really, they don't die. They can't. They are wound up, charged with enough energy, enough juice, to carry them for seventy, seventy-five years. But a bottled bolt of lightning came from the electrical outlet and poured across the red fire truck. It crackled through Mikey's fingertips and stole him away, even though we were all watching him and doors were locked and the gate was up.

Teri screams.

*Ohgodohgodohgodohgodohgodohgodohgodohgodoh*

Time speeds up again.

Teri sits on the floor, her legs stuck out in front of her like a broken doll, her dead Mikey in her arms. I am a shrieking ghost, seeing everything, unseen.

Daddy runs up the steps, Ms. Cummings runs up the steps, the hard hats run up the steps. They peel Teri away from her Mikey, pry the baby from her hands. They lay him out on the hard floor, his arms thrown carelessly over his head like he wants to be picked up and swung around, spun until he's dizzy.

Check his pulse, breathe into his mouth, pizza breath, grape-juice stained. Push on his chest, one-two-three, one-two-three, knead-the-bread, back-from-the-dead. Breathe. Breathe.

Broken-doll Teri lies forgotten in the corner. I float across the room and settle next to her. Her hands are frozen into the holy shape of Mikey's head and his chin. I touch her elbow. I pet her shoulder. Her body feels empty. Neither of us is really here. We left when time stopped.

Push on his chest, one-two-three, one-two-three, knead-the-bread, back-from-the-dead. Breathe. Breathe. My father and my teacher trade positions; you push, I'll breathe. Their hands are so big for the little body, their shoulders touch, a frantic dance. They read each other, finger Braille on the boy's dirty skin. He looks at her. She looks at him. Eye talk. Push on his chest, one-two-three, one-two-three, knead-the-bread, back-from-the-dead. Breathe. Breathe.

Faces hover in the doorway: Sara, Mitchell, Travis. Nameless adults. Pete performs crowd control, sweeps them back down the stairs. Nothing you can do, nothing to see here, out of the way, we'll let you know.

A fat pearl of sweat rolls down the side of my father's face, slips past the lines around his mouth, his Sunday night stubble, and falls—splash—onto Mikey's glass forehead.

Red lights chase the shadows around the walls. An ambulance howls and skids into the driveway. My father's mouth moves, moves, but I can't hear him. The noise inside Teri has stopped. I hold on to her elbow tighter to keep her from floating out the window.

The heroes run up the steps, *thump-thump-thump*, snapping on filmy plastic gloves. The emergency rituals begin. They check Mikey's pupils and listen to Mikey's heart. It's not talking to us, not even a whisper. Scissors *riiiiiip* . . .

his shirt is gone . . . the air so cold for a tiny chest, count his ribs, one-two-three, grease the paddles—

"Clear."

Electricity rips through the little bones, the pint boxes of blood, the Mikey.

Teri howls.

Nothing, no line, no pulse, no spike.

"Clear!"

We can't catch him. Mikey's heart is gone, shut down and cold. Teri rocks from side to side, a boulder teetering on the edge of the cliff. I hold her shoulders, slippery, desperate, to keep her from crashing. She howls louder than an ambulance, louder than a thousand screaming crows, eyes rolled back in her head so she doesn't have to watch the worst of everything, this end.

They inject something in the soft skin inside her elbow, the crook of her arm where she balanced her son's sweaty head. I understand now. She keeps telling me: "He's my son, my son, my baby, my boy."

# Part 3 | Gas

$$C_p \text{ } steam = 1.8 \text{ } \frac{J}{g^\circ C}$$

**"Organic substances exist as molecules with covalent bonds holding the individual atoms together."**

—*ARCO Everything You Need to Score*
*High on AP Chemistry*, 3rd Edition

# 8.0 | Photoelectrons

*SAFETY TIP: Some chemicals deserve special attention because of potential instability.*

The TV news crews arrive as Mikey is being carried out of the house. The lights from the cameras give me a sunburn. Teri is escorted to the back of the ambulance and helped up the step by two EMTs. They want her to lie down, but she refuses. She lifts Mikey's body from the second stretcher and cradles him in her lap. The camera operators adjust their lenses for the close-up and I think I have to scream. Someone is grabbing my arms, but the light is so bright, I can't tell who it is.

Teri turns slightly and her hair falls forward, shielding her face and Mikey from the eyes and the lenses and the lights. The EMTs hop in the back and the ambulance driver closes the door. The cameras turn and follow the ambulance as it rolls down the driveway, then pulls out onto the road, red lights flashing. There is no siren.

"Are you okay?" Mitch whispers in my ear. "Do you want to go home?"

The camera operators cut the lights and the night jumps back into photo negative relief.

"Not yet," I say.

My father and Ms. Cummings help Mrs. Litch into the back of the Godmobile. Ms. Cummings buckles the seat belt over Mrs. Litch's lap. Dad gets in the driver's seat and backs down the driveway to follow the ambulance. Mrs. Litch stares dead ahead.

The police take notes and photos, their flashes bouncing back and forth in time, measuring and recording until they finally put away their pencils. They murmur into their mikes. The other volunteers, the hard hats, the adults, wander offstage like actors who have forgotten their lines. They head for their cars and they drive to their houses, where they will check to make sure their own children are breathing.

"Do you want to go home?" Mitch asks me.

"Not yet," I say.

We stay. My friends and Toby and me, we stay. Sara unearths a handful of candles. We light every single one of them and stick them on the floor of what was going to be the playroom, directly below the big-boy room, because it is very dark in Teri Litch's house. We sit on the floor, between the candles and the wall, five monkeys in a line: Toby, me, Mitch, Sara, Travis. The light licks the yellow handprints Mikey left on the wall.

God.

Toby leans against me. I sag against Mitch. Sara moves, Travis shifts, and the five of us dissolve into a pool, one heart beating. Toby is warm. I'm shivering. He clutches my waist. I press my cheek against Mitch's shoulder. Mitch grabs the back of my neck. In our shadows, Sara's hair flows from Travis's head, his legs grow out of her body. Travis reaches out and drapes an arm across my brother's shaking shoulders. We take turns breathing.

They cry and their tears roll on the wood floor. My eyes are dry, frozen behind my contacts. I crawl into a candle flame until it becomes a whiteout, the color of hospital walls and bandages and wax bodies. It feels as if my contacts are peeling off. I close my eyes and rub them with my fists. The light explodes like a broken kaleidoscope with all the gritty bits draining away. I untangle myself from the circle and wrap my arms around my knees.

"It's our fault. We let him go," I say. "We weren't watching."

Mitch's head snaps up. "Don't say that, Kate. Don't even think it."

"She can't help what she thinks," Sara says.

Mitch stands up. "It wasn't our fault. Don't feel guilty."

Toby wipes his face on his shirt and slides closer to the line of candles. "You know what the worst part was?" he whispers.

"What, Tobe?" I ask.

"The way his arms flopped when she picked him up, like he was made of rags."

The candle flames blow another whiteout across my eyes.

"If anyone is at fault, it's that inspector." Mitch crosses his arms over his chest. "He left the job site with a dangerous hazard out in the open. He could be arrested. At the very least, he should be fired."

"What?" I ask.

Sara frowns. "Who cares?"

"Somebody should care," Mitch says. "This could be a massive lawsuit."

I shiver again. "I'm going to pretend you didn't say that. Nothing matters right now. Nothing."

My brother leans forward and waves his fingers through a flame, testing the speed at which he'll get burned. The heat crinkles the hair on the back of his hand

Mitch paces at the edge of the shadows. "It does matter. It matters a lot. A kid died here. Right here."

"Dude, settle down," Travis says. "We know. It was an accident."

"Accidents don't happen," Mitch say. "Someone is always responsible."

Toby presses his thumb into the soft wax at the top of a candle. He flattens the rim and sculpts it into a rose. Molten wax runs down the back of his giant hands and hardens. The light reflects up against the angles of his face, catching in the fuzz above his top lip.

"I don't want to talk about this now," Sara says.

Mitch turns in the shadows. "How can you not talk about it?"

"I just want to be quiet."

"You can't be quiet. He's dead."

Travis stands up. "Chill. Take it easy."

Toby moves to the next candle. I pull myself to my feet and walk to the collection of paint cans in the corner. I pick one up, carry it back to the light, and pry off the lid. Yellow; the color of dried chrysanthemum petals. When Toby was tiny, he had a jar of yellow fingerpaint this exact same shade. I would cover the kitchen floor with sheets of blank paper, and we would paint with our fingers and hands and elbows and knees and toes.

I stick my right pointer finger in the paint. It's cold and yogurt-thick. I dip my fingers in one by one and stir slowly, counterclockwise. I cup my hand in the yellow, then raise it and let paint roll down my arm. I dip in again, then stand up and fling my hand toward the wall, like a magic wand. The paint flies, glistens, lands, a perfect sun-splatter above the handprints that Mikey left.

Toby looks up with a gasp.

Sara smiles. She takes off her rings and bracelets, and braids her hair out of harm's way. Travis opens two more cans, red and blue. I plunge my left hand in, bring it out dripping threads of rich blue sorrow. I throw a handful of blue at the wall.

"No," Mitchell "Heartless" Pangborn says. "You can't throw paint at walls. It's not your house."

My contacts are working again. I can see his words hang in the air, then crash to the floor. He is standing so far away from the light that it is hard to make out the lines of his face. His hands are locked in the dark behind him.

"If you don't like it, you can leave," I say.

He walks out without another word. When the door slams, the candlelight jumps.

Toby dips his fingertip in the blue can and paints the figure of a tiny man on the wall. I throw more blue at the wall, leaving lines of color on the floor, on my sneakers and legs. Travis paints tiny monsters flying around the window frame. Sara puts a yellow handprint by the light switch. Mitch's car starts up. He backs down the driveway slowly, then lays rubber on the road.

I stand back and observe my masterpiece. I am so not an artist. Does it matter? This wall, this house, it's all coming down. I bet they bulldoze it and sell the land.

Sara ties her T-shirt up under her bra and Travis paints a face on her belly. She draws a flower on his bald head. My brother finds a couple of Mikey's trucks in the living room. He dips an eighteen-wheeler onto the surface of the red paint and runs the truck along the wall, leaving wet tire tracks. He hands me the moving truck. I dip it in blue. We work together until the candles burn out.

Teri and my father return to our house a little after midnight. Mr. Spock and I are watching *Star Trek* reruns with Toby tucked under the quilt on the couch behind us. The front door opens and slams shut, and Teri shuffles past me without a word. On her left wrist, she's wearing a plastic hospital bracelet along with my watch. She heads up the stairs to my bedroom.

I join Dad in the kitchen. He takes a beer out of the fridge and sucks it down while I wait at the kitchen table. When the beer is gone, he sets the bottle in the recycling bin. He leans against the sink and recites softly, bringing me up-to-date.

To summarize:

1. Teri is sedated. She'll be staying with us for an unspecified period of time.

2. Mrs. Litch is even more sedated. She's at Betty's house.

3. Mikey died of a massive electrical shock.

4. Mikey will be buried on Tuesday, in the morning. The Litches want to get it over with.

5. Mikey didn't know what hit him.

Dad gulps back a sob. He holds his breath for a minute, then exhales slowly. His eyes are watery and old.

"I'm sorry, Kate."

I don't know what to say.

He massages his temples and grimaces. I take his migraine medicine out of the cupboard by the sink, hand it to him, and pour him a glass of water. He tosses back the pill and drinks the water. "Thanks."

"Can I ask you a question?"

He nods slightly.

"Mikey's father—it was Mr. Litch, wasn't it? Charlie."

Dad turns on the hot water and carefully washes the glass before answering. "Quite possibly. Probably. I'm going to try and get Teri into counseling, see if there is anything I can do to help." He takes a shaky breath. "How's your brother? How are you doing?"

"Toby was kind of freaked out, but he's sleeping now. I'm okay."

He dries the glass and returns it to the cupboard. "You should get some sleep, too. Go on upstairs now. And turn out the light, will you? It's bothering my eyes."

I hit the switch as I leave the room. He opens another beer in the dark.

Teri Litch has no intention of sleeping. As I walk into my bedroom, she is trying to escape out the window.

I grab her arm. "What the hell are you doing?"

"Go away." She shakes me off and tries again.

Given her luck, she'll fracture every bone in her body. I put my arms around her waist and try to pull her to the bed. "You . . . have . . . to . . . stay . . . here."

She releases the window frame and looks down at me. "Let go."

"No way. You're trying to kill yourself."

She steps backward and pushes me off. "Not killing myself."

"What do you call jumping out the window?"

"I just wanna go home," she whispers.

I flick on the overhead light and blink. She's not wearing her glasses. Her eyes are so puffy I can't see the pupils. There are scratches on her face, a bandage on her forearm.

"They gave you drugs, Teri. You need to sleep. You're not thinking clearly."

She makes a flapping mouth motion with her fingers. "Blah. Blah. Blah."

I move between her and the window. "Seriously, you can't go back there, not tonight. There's no heat."

"So?" The springs squeak as she sits on the edge of my bed.

"So stay here." (Ask me to drive you to Betty's house so you can stay with your mom, please, please, please.) "Stay here and rest."

She shakes her head from side to side, her hair swinging gently. "Nope. Nope. Nope. Where he died, the exact spot. That's where I'm sleeping."

No way. Even I can see the mental health implications in that. "Tomorrow. When the sun is up and you're feeling better. Dad will go with you. I will, too, if you want. But you can't go back now. I'm serious. Teri? Listen to me. Sit down. Come back here. Teri! You can't—"

She closes the door behind her.

Damn.


## 8.1 ▌ Residual Matter

By the time I get down to the Litches' house, Teri is upstairs, sitting cross-legged on the floor where Mikey died. The moon is swimming through the window, casting silk shadows. She has stripped down to her bra, underpants, and mismatched socks. A semicircle of toy cars and trucks arcs in front of her; the half-empty toy basket is in her lap. First in the line is a fire truck.

"Teri. Teri?"

She doesn't answer. Her eyes are focused on a spot beyond the cars. I drape the blanket I brought over her shoulders and lay the pillows on the floor beside her. The air is thick with moonlight and the smell of Teri. She breathes in and out slowly, a wet, reluctant tide.

I'm trespassing on holy ground.

The boards creak as I make for the door. Teri's arm shoots out toward me, her fingers splayed open.

"Do you want me to stay?" I ask.

Nothing. Did she hear me? Is she freaking out on whatever the hospital injected?

"Teri." My voice is too loud. "What do you want me to do? Stay?"

She slides the toy basket across the floor.

"Suit yourself," she slurs.

Another beat of silence. The house creaks and the air quivers with Litch lies and secrets and memories.

I sit behind her, my back against hers. I take the ice cream truck out of the basket and set it in line. Next comes the police car, then the Jeep, the motorboat, the cement truck, the bulldozer. One by one the paint-chipped, dented, wheel-free vehicles of Mikey Litch line up until at last the basket is empty and the circle is finished.

I can feel Teri twist as she looks to her right and to her left, making sure I completed the job properly. She settles back with a grunt and leans against me. The ridge of her backbone is thick, like she has hunks of granite instead of vertebrae. When we are balanced back-to-back, covered by the blanket and encircled by toys, her gray hand appears again, slipping blindly toward mine. Our fingers weave together. Her hand is so hot, I can feel blisters forming. It's like holding on to a kerosene heater, hearing the sizzle and pop of burning flesh. Paint peels off my skin and drops to the floor, drops between the cracks. But I don't let go.

# 9.0 | Radioactive

Sunday is a foggy day. Teri refuses breakfast and asks Dad to drive her to Betty's house so she can see her mother. Ms. Cummings stops in after church and says Toby and I are in shock. She makes us pudding and leaves.

I want to play Hearts, but Toby keeps falling asleep. He could have a viral form of narcolepsy, or maybe he's suffering from exposure to the paint fumes last night. I take the phone off the hook so he can get some rest.

I look at my homework, but it doesn't make any sense. I take out my contacts and put on my glasses and it doesn't help.

I think maybe I should do some laundry.

I think maybe I should check my e-mail.

I think maybe I should brainstorm about my MIT appeal.

But all I can do is to watch cartoons, all day and half the night. It's really foggy out.

Teri stumbles into my bedroom at one o'clock on Monday morning and wakes me up. She has walked from

Betty's house to mine, with a stop at The Moon for a beer or two or eight.

I leave a note for Toby and Dad on the kitchen table and drive Teri to her house. We sleep on the floor of Mikey's room again. It's even colder than the night before.

# IO.O ▎ Phase Transition

*SAFETY TIP: Wear lab coat when handling corrosive or flammable substances.*

There is no point in going to school on Monday. No point whatsoever.

Teri has other ideas. She shoves me awake at dawn. "We're going to be late," she says, pulling on her dirty clothes.

I rub my cheek. I toppled over in the night and slept on the cement truck. "We don't have to go to school. Dad will call and explain."

She pulls on her jeans. "Why would I want to stay around here?"

Because you're in shock, you need counseling, you need Prozac and many other drugs, your son is dead, you need to cry, you need more sleep, you need to eat something, you need to plan a funeral, you need to deal with all this shit.

"Fine," I say, trying to stand up. "Let's go to school."

When we get to my house, Teri walks straight to Bert and lets herself in on the passenger's side. I duck in the house to change quickly and grab my books. I tell Dad what's up and remind him to give Toby his meds. The recycling bin is full of beer bottles and Dad is moving slowly. No comment.

Teri doesn't say a word during the drive to school. She follows me through the parking lot and stands patiently in line to get through security. I show my ID and pass through the gates without setting off any alarms. Teri doesn't even reach for her wallet. She just walks through, head down.

"Don't you need to see her identification?" I ask the security guard.

"Everybody knows Teri," the guard dog says. "Move along, please."

The bell rings and the crowd in the lobby streams off down the halls. We pass *Student Body*, the bizarre sculpture Mr. Freeman's art class built. Sure enough, someone ripped off the heart. The jockstrap, too.

Teri failed to mention the part where she planned to accompany me to my classes. Ms. Cummings's eyebrow arches up when we walk into chem, but she doesn't say a word. Teri takes a seat at the empty lab table by the fume hood. When she lays her head down, my necklace slips out from the collar of her shirt and the gold heart pings once on the table. She falls asleep instantly.

My friends, enemies, and competitors whisper the expected questions and toss me notes, but I am a rock; I say nothing. In fact, I don't do anything, either. Ms. Cummings gets it. She calls Diana up to her desk to make excuses for me and gives her instructions on how she can get through today's lab single-handed. Diana comes back and tells me she's sorry about everything. "Everything" is a very big word.

The class gets to work. They are studying the rate of reaction influenced by the presence of catalysts and inhibitors and a bunch of other stuff. My brain refuses to tune in to the Chemistry Channel this morning. I should have taken a shower. I tilt my chair back (flagrant rule-breaking) and study the holes left in the ceiling by a generation of pencil points. Nasty little thoughts ping-pong inside me.

I wonder where Mikey's body is.

I wonder what Teri is thinking. She must be thinking, even if she's asleep. I bet her mind is in hyper-drive. Or maybe she jettisoned her warp core and is adrift.

I wonder what she's going to do now. Everything has changed, right? If it hasn't, that would be even more awful.

I wonder if they washed Mikey's feet. He had the dirtiest feet of any kid I've ever known.

I wonder why MIT rejected me.

I am so sick. I am scum. That's why MIT rejected me. I failed the sick scum test.

I have no future. I'm going to live at home, care for my aging father, and sell condoms at the pharmacy. If they don't fire me because I am sick scum. Maybe I can get a job at Superfresh, working for Ed.

God, I'm cold.

What is Teri going to do? What was she going to do before everything happened? College? The army?

What about her mother—can she live alone?

Teri will join the army, rise through the ranks, and command the U.S. troops in the Pacific. She'll live in Hawaii. I will live at home, care for my aging father and her aging, blind, diabetic mother, and sell day-old bread at the Superfresh.

Sick, pathetic, overwrought scum. And my quads hurt. And my Achilles tendon, and that stupid pec muscle is bothering me again, probably from carrying around . . .

Suddenly the class is empty, except for Ms. Cummings at her desk, watching Teri, who is standing next to me. Class is over.

"Wake up," Teri says. "Where do we go next?"

"We eat."

## 10.1 ▌ Titanium

We have to walk past the football team in the cafeteria. The guys don't say anything to Teri, even though she glares at each one, straight in the eyes, daring them, egging them on. They must have seen it on the news. Everybody knows. Everything. Every stinking little thing.

Once we are past them, Teri's shoulders sag as if the air has been let out of her. I can't believe she's standing, much less has the energy to walk or dare the team to fight her again. She is made of titanium. Titanium doesn't tarnish easily. It doesn't conduct electricity so well either, considering it's a metal.

Sara and Travis are waiting with four coffee cups and a greasy bag of doughnuts. Like Ms. Cummings, they're surprised to see Teri, but they cover it with a polite "Hey" and "What's up?"

"Where's Pangborn?" I ask.

"He's not here," Sara says. "Teri, you want some coffee?"

Teri lifts her head. "Yeah. Thanks."

Sara gets up and jogs to the lunch line. Teri stares at the swirl of yellow paint on Travis's forehead.

"We finished painting the playroom," I explain. "The other night after . . . after you left. It's a little sloppy. We'll go back and paint it over. When you want. If you want."

She closes her eyes. *Shut up, Malone. Just leave her alone.*

Sara comes back with an extra cup. She carefully pours coffee from each of our cups into Teri's until we all have the same amount. Then she pushes the cup across the table and says quietly, "We have glazed doughnuts."

Teri takes a shaky breath and opens her eyes. "I like glazed."

I open the bag and offer it to her. She reaches in and takes one, then breaks it in two and hands the small half to me. I dunk it quickly in my coffee and take a bite. The icing melts and softens on my tongue, sweet and warm and delicate.

Teri blows on her coffee, sips, then eats. She isn't wearing her glasses. How come I didn't notice that before? The last time I saw her wearing them was that night, I think. In the ambulance? Before the ambulance? The swelling around her eyes has gone down a bit. There are dried lines of salt on her face. I overdunk and slop coffee on the table. I take another bite. When was the last time I had a glazed?

Travis yawns. He puts four packets of sugar in his coffee, stirs it with a pencil, and gulps down half of it.

"You get any sleep?" he asks Teri.

"Enough," she says. "You?"

He smiles. "Not enough."

"Do you want me to go home and get your glasses?" I ask.

"I like it blurry," Teri says.

Travis nods. "Exactly."

That was good, an almost-normal conversation. She doesn't look like she's going postal or anything. Maybe as long as she stays in school, she can pretend it's still a normal day, and she'll go home, and Mikey will be there. If it hurts me to think about that, I can't begin to imagine what it feels like for her.

Sara pokes my hand with a coffee stirrer. "You should call Mitch."

"Why?"

"Trav called his house, and his mom says he doesn't want to talk to anyone. So you should call him."

Travis nods. Teri is lost in her coffee cup.

"He'll turn up," I say. "You know him." The last time Mitchell missed a day of school, he was in first grade and had the chicken pox. He's been gunning for the district attendance record ever since.

"His mom said he was acting strange," Trav says. "He was cleaning."

"Cleaning?"

"He was so weird . . . " Sara swallows hard and studies her nails, "you know, when we were painting."

Travis licks his finger and uses it to pick up the spilled sugar on the table. "Both of you guys have been acting weird, if you ask me. Too much geek pressure."

"It's like you're having a symbiotic meltdown," Sara says.

"They need sex," Travis tells her.

Teri acts like she doesn't hear a word of this. She reaches for what should have been Mitch's cup of coffee and drinks from it.

I brush the doughnut crumbs into my hand. "Stop being melodramatic. No one is having a meltdown."

"Call it what you want. Pangborn is changing," Travis says. "He's been watching that damn Golf Channel. It's polluting his soul."

"And you guys have been fighting. Aren't you worried?" Sara asks.

"I have other things to worry about right now," I say.

Teri sets the empty cup on the table. She is still wearing her hospital bracelet and my watch.

■　■　■

## 10.2 ▮ Freezing-Point Depression

We're trapped in a wormhole the rest of the day. My body is in slow motion, dragging through classes that look like video clips transmitted through a lousy modem connection. The memories of the weekend, they're all piped through a DSL line. Teri walks next to me, Teri sits next to me, wordless. I reroute us through the halls to avoid going near the pre-school classroom.

English—blah, blah, blah. No Mitch. Ms. Devlin still thinks understanding Greek mythology is the key to happiness. If you ask me, Theresa Litch is a living, breathing Greek tragedy.

AP Euro—The Balkan Wars (1912–13) helped create World War I. Why do they think we care about this? Teri spends the class writing in my notebooks. She rips out the pages and stuffs them in her pocket. Is this how she should be reacting? Maybe I should call my father.

Calculus—Now I know I'm trapped in an alternate universe. Calculus has become pointless. Still no Mitchell Pangborn. My antennae are wriggling.

Gym—It's raining. We are supposed to watch a video about the importance of stretching. Teri and I sleep on the wrestling mats.

Study Hall—Napping, Part II.

AP French—who gives a *merde*?

I don't take Teri to track practice, though I am dying for

a long, sweaty run. I have to take her back to the real world. Plus I'm still sore.

There is a funeral director in our kitchen, Mrs. Litch sitting by his side. He has a giant binder open on the table, a binder filled with pictures of caskets. He doesn't look like a funeral director. He looks normal. This is a terrifying thought. You could walk past somebody like this in the mall, and you would never know he handles dead bodies all day. What other anonymous aliens are out there messing with us?

Teri pulls out a chair. The legs screech against the floor. She sits down and reaches for the book of caskets. I am so out of here.

Dad catches me as I am flying down the hall. He is wearing a black suit with a white shirt and the gray knit tie Mom bought him years ago. It is knotted high against his Adam's apple.

"Thanks for helping out with Teri," he says.

"I'm not helping. She just follows me. How are they going to pay for a casket? They cost thousands of—"

He holds up his hand. "It's taken care of. Someone called and offered to take care of the expenses. They saw what happened on the news."

Why do these generous mystery donors always wait until a kid dies before they show up? Where were they when Teri's father was coming into her bedroom, and beating the crap out of her mother? I'd love to ask Dad, but all I'd get would be the Patient Look, the You Don't Understand the Ways of the World, Little Girl Look, and if I got that now, I'd spontaneously combust into a million fragments of blonde hair and bone and skin.

"Maybe you should go in and sit with her," he says.

"No way. I can't. I can't look at those things. I have to make a phone call, Dad. In private."

## 10.3 ▌ Transmutation

This is perverse, but I can't help myself. I can't think about Mikey, not for another second. I can't think about Teri or Mitchell or my father or anyone else. My hands seek out the phone and punch in the ten-digit number, plus one, for long distance. I have it memorized.

"Hello? My name is Colleen Malone," I say, invoking the name of the long dead. "Class of '84. I'd like to speak to someone about my daughter's application. Kate—Kathleen M. Malone."

"Was she rejected?" asks MIT.

Swallow hard, old girl.

"Yes, she was. We were wondering about an appeal, or if . . . if someone could tell us why you turned her down. She's heartbroken."

"I understand," purrs MIT. "It's a hard thing to go through."

After a couple of minutes on hold, sharing my Social

Security number and other useless information, more time on hold, they finally patch the ghost of my mother through to somebody with an answer.

"Your daughter is very intelligent—no question about it. High grades in advanced placement classes, plays a sport, a few clubs."

"She won a national science competition."

"I see. She'll have no problem getting into any number of schools."

"But she's had her heart set on MIT since fourth grade."

"I am very sorry, Mrs. Malone." The intercom buzzes.

"No, no, no." I shake my head like a two-year-old. MIT is slipping away from me. I can feel it. "Is it the money?" I ask. "I know, I know, we're poorer than dirt. But she can work. I'll . . . I'll take another job, wash dishes, wash windows. Kate can work, too; she's a good worker. We'll do anything."

"It's not the money, Mrs. Malone. We don't make our decisions based on the size of the applicant's bank account."

"Then what did she do wrong?"

MIT pauses. "There's a boy entering this fall who has already patented genetic therapy on fruit flies. We have a girl who wrote her own translation program from Chinese into Somalian. They bring that extra something, that oomph."

"Oomph?"

"Oomph. Your daughter is smart, Mrs. Malone. But she is missing something, that something extra. And frankly, her essays were weak. I recommend she work on her writing skills. I know you love her very much and you want the best place for her. MIT is not the best place for her right now."

The intercom interrupts again.

"She would be an asset to your campus," I try.

"I'm sorry. I have an appointment now." The MIT mask slips back into place. I can hear the elastic band twang, vibrate, then go still. "Good luck, Kate. Good-bye."

Nobody is home at Sara's house. I back down her driveway carefully and head for the other side of her development. I'm terrified that if I take my eyes off the road for even one second I'll go out of control and run down an old lady or sideswipe a police car. Five blocks later I park on the street, get out, shut my door, and lock it. Then I unlock and open it and double-check that I turned off my headlights. Double-triple-check that I have the keys in my hand. Close the door. Lock the door. Keys still in hand. Check.

Mrs. Pangborn opens her front door while talking into a telephone headset. "They have to remove it, it's in the contract. I don't care how much it costs. My client refuses to take possession while there is a two-ton statue of copulating Greek gods on the patio. Would you want to eat breakfast next to that thing?"

She waves her fingers at me and smiles. "Hang on, Anne, I've got another call."

She presses the hold button at her waist and gives me a quick hug that smells like Victoria's Secret lotion. "Kate. I heard all about it. You poor thing."

"I'm okay."

"Do you want to stay for dinner? I won't pester you with questions, I promise."

This is the first time I've seen Mrs. Pangborn with my contacts in. With my glasses on, it was always easy to see what it would be like to cook Christmas dinner with her, to invite her to my college graduation, thank her for my bridal shower, drop off the grandkids, and other assorted nonsense. With the contacts in, I can't see any of it.

"We're having salmon," she says. "I can make a dill sauce."

I blink. "Thanks, but I can't. There is a lot going on at home. Is Mitch around?"

She rolls her eyes. "In his room. I don't know how you finally did it, but thank you. He told us last night."

"He told you what?"

"He's finally going to be practical about college. He wants to study international economics, then go to business school. Thank God!"

The red light by her hold button blinks.

"I've got to finish this call, honey. Go on upstairs. You're welcome to stay if you change your mind. We're eating in half an hour." She clicks the hold button again. "Anne? I'm back. Yeah, another settlement nightmare. Do they ever end?"

The Pangborns have always assumed that because Mitchell is a straight-A student and major Eagle Scout, he doesn't have hormones. They just can't imagine their

Precious Baby having a lustful moment. Or fast hands. Or a wet tongue.

I walk up the stairs, head down the hall, and knock on the door with the Harvard banner. He grunts. I enter.

Mitchell's room is usually like Toby's, a breeding ground for bacteria and nasty ideas. Hence my shock. The curtains are tied back, and the windows are shiny clean. I can see his floor. (It's covered in dark blue carpet—who knew?) His bed is made up with a quilt and pillows on it. The only things on his desk, his *dusted* desk, are his computer monitor and keyboard. The bookcase is actually filled with books, upright and spines out. Soccer trophies shine in parade formation on the top of the bookcase.

Mitch is wearing a T-shirt and sweats, sitting in the middle of his floor sorting through a mountain of papers. Some are placed in file folders, but it looks like most have been chucked in the black garbage bag next to him. He's got his earphones on and is bobbing back and forth, humming off-key. I have to move into his line of sight to get his attention.

He takes off the earphones and stands up. "What's wrong? You look terrible."

I kick off my sneakers, pull back the covers, and get into his bed.

"Kate? Are you okay?"

I close my eyes and shake my head. "I'm losing it, Pangborn."

"Define 'losing it.'"

I pull the sheet up around my neck. "I called MIT and pretended to be my mom."

He turns off the CD player. "Why?"

"I thought they made a mistake, let in the wrong Kate Malone."

"And?"

I look up at him, shielding my eyes with my hand. Black spots dance in the air. He is standing with his back to the windows. The sunlight flares around his edges like a corona. It puts his face in shadow. "I can't see you."

He locks the door and crawls under the covers with me. I lift my head so he can lay one arm under it, and he pulls me close. He smells like boy. I close my eyes again. The spots are still there, red now instead of black.

"Do you think I'm freaking out?" I whisper. "I think I'm lost. Somebody switched the road signs and I'm stuck with an old map."

Mitch places his finger on my lips. "Shh . . . Be quiet."

I can feel his pulse under the skin of his neck. Slower, Malone. Stop running. My heart trips over itself again, then settles into a soft, steady rhythm. I could fall asleep here, melt into his chest. He'd keep the world on the other side of that door if I asked him, he'd cradle my head and keep me warm.

He kisses my forehead. I tilt my face and pull him close for a gentle kiss. His arms tighten, he presses against me, and the kiss gets hard and deep. He tastes like he's been eating rodents.

I pull back and make a face. "Yuck! What's that?"

His chuckle shakes the headboard. "Beef jerky. Sorry. I didn't think you'd be crawling in my bed today."

I wave the air between us. "It's fetid."

"All right, I won't breathe on you." He rolls on his back. "Come here."

I lay my head on his chest and he strokes my hair. I press my ear against his shirt. His heart beats lazy like a rocking chair. This is a good place to freeze time, right here, this very second.

"So, what did MIT say to your pretend mom?"

A telephone rings. Mrs. Pangborn's heels clatter across the tile floor in the foyer. Her voice echoes up the stairwell, chattering about nothing and nothing and nothing. She is a fab saleswoman.

"Kate?" he asks softly.

I smooth his shirt over his chest. It's a new shirt, I haven't seen it before.

"I, um, I lack 'oomph,' that's what the MIT god told my mom." Spots dance in front of my eyes again. "I am one of a million wannabe geeks—great, just not great enough. And my essays sucked."

"Shit."

"Yeah."

"So . . . you're not going."

"I'm not going. And look, I know things are a little weird between us right now, but please don't make me talk. I just need you to hold me because it sort of feels like gravity doesn't work anymore."

He pulls me close.

"Not that tight," I say. "I still need to breathe."

"Sorry. Is that better?"

"Great, thanks."

Mrs. Pangborn's voice moves from the foyer to the kitchen. I can picture her taking the salmon out of the refrigerator. She'll smell it to make sure it's fresh. She'll turn on the oven, spray a pan with no-fat, butter-tasting chemicals, and wash the vegetables.

Mitch's voice rumbles deep in his chest. "Which safety are you going to take?"

I have not been nice enough to Mrs. Pangborn. She offered to go shopping for a prom dress with me a few weeks ago, and I blew her off. That was bitchy of me.

"Kate?"

"I said I didn't want to talk."

"You don't have a choice. This is your life. Which safety?"

I curl into a ball and pull the sheet up over my head. "I don't have a safety."

"What did you say? Speak up."

"I only applied to one school. MIT. I thought I was a sure thing."

"So I was right? You never wrote those essays, that's why you wouldn't show them to me?"

I pause to swallow the jerky taste. "Much as it kills me to admit it, yes, you were right."

My boyfriend, my enemy, my lust lies still for a moment. "What does your dad say?"

"He doesn't know. You're the only person who does."

His heart is beating faster. Mine is about to propel me out of the bed. "If you call me stupid or laugh—"

He takes a deep breath. "Man, it's hot in here." He stands up, crosses the room, and opens the windows over his desk. Seen through the cotton weave of the sheet, his edges are blurry. He leans forward to look outside. "So . . . no college in September. That sucks. Really. I'm sorry."

The oven door bangs in the kitchen. I bet we're having spaghetti at my house. Spaghetti and bread. I bet Teri isn't hungry, not after choosing a casket. It's funny, the funeral director had his casket pictures in a heavy-duty, three-ring binder, the kind you use at school that would last all the way to June if you're lucky, the kind you fill with handouts that have carefully punched holes in the left margin, holes that you reinforce with sticky white circles because you don't want to lose any handouts because you never know what you are going to be tested on.

"What are you going to do?" he asks.

I shrug, but he can't see it. "I'll come up with something. I guess I have to, don't I?"

"Yep."

Whatever is out that window sure must be fascinating.

"What's up with you changing your major?" I ask.

"Mom told you, huh?" He turns around. "They're thrilled."

I take the sheet off my head. My hair crackles with static electricity. "Yeah, but economics?"

"Yep."

I sit up and cross my legs. "What happened to history? You love history."

"Waste of time."

"I'm calling the tabloids. You're a clone. The real Mitchell Pangborn has been abducted by aliens."

"Nope. This is me. I'm finally growing up, I guess. Time to deal with real life."

"But Mitch, you're going be a college professor. You don't like dealing with real life."

"I changed my mind."

I wave my hand in the air. "Hello? When did this happen?"

"When they put Mikey's body in the ambulance." He looks out the window again. "I've never seen a dead person before. Well, I did on TV, but that doesn't count. One minute he was there, he was running around, his nose was snotty, and then . . . then I heard Teri scream and you scream. Everything got crazy. They put him in the ambulance. Farting around with ancient history is a waste of time. I want to do something useful, something that counts."

I pull a pillow into my lap. "International economics wouldn't have saved Mikey."

He picks up a pile of papers from the carpet and shoves them in the trash bag. "No, but it's practical. Why are you arguing with me? You've been telling me history is a waste of time for years."

"I think I was wrong. I think you should study some-thing that you love."

Mrs. Pangborn calls up the stairs. "Dinner in ten minutes!"

"I'll learn to love it. Are you staying for dinner? Mom's been asking where you've been."

"I can't. I already told her. I want to see how Teri is doing." I take my keys and a pack of gum out of my purse. I unwrap two sticks of wintergreen and put both of them in my mouth.

Mitch shivers once. "It got cold again. God, I hate spring. Blizzard, heat wave, blizzard, heat wave." He shuts the win-dow and pulls the curtains together. His edges blur again.

I sling my purse over my shoulder. "Teri and I slept at her house last night. In Mikey's room."

"Why?"

"She wanted to."

"You can't let her boss you around like that, Kate. You have to take control."

He gives me another beef jerky kiss before opening the door. "Thanks for coming over. It's kind of cool that you were worried about me."

My mask slips back into place. I can hear the elastic band twang, vibrate, then go still. I smile. "Thanks for lis-tening about the college thing. You really helped a lot."

When I return home, Dad is sitting on the front porch with Ms. Cummings. The two empty teacups and a plate with cookie crumbs on the table are her touch. If he were alone, it'd be a beer bottle and an empty potato chip bag.

"There's pizza inside," Dad says.

"Did Toby eat?"

"He's over at a friend's house. I thought it would do him good to get away for a little bit."

"What about Teri?" I ask.

"Watching television," Ms. Cummings says. "She said the two of you were going to sleep at her house again."

Well, no, actually I want my own bed, all to myself with clean sheets and no Litch odors or ghosts.

"Yeah," I say. "Whatever. How is she?"

"Quiet. The funeral is all planned. Everything is ready. " A rusty pickup truck barreling down the road backfires loudly. The sound makes Dad wince.

"Did you take your migraine medicine at dinner?" I ask.

"I forgot."

"I'll get it for you." I pick up the cookie plate and teacups. Dad stands up to get the door for me.

"Is Mitchell Pangborn all right?" Ms. Cummings asks. "I heard he missed school today. He almost had the record."

"Yeah, it's a shame." I pause on the threshold. "He lost it."

# 11.0 | Alpha Decay

*SAFETY TIP: Fire-polish all rough glass edges.*

It is Tuesday. The sun is supposed to shine. There is something obscene about burying a tiny body on a spring day that smells like lilacs.

I'm fighting something viral. It's winning. I've got chills, my head hurts, and I want to heave. My eyes are so irritated and dry that I can't get my contacts in. I shouldn't have gone running last night.

I slip the black dress over my head, reach around, and pull up the zipper. A black velvet headband keeps my hair out of my face. I put on my glasses. A perfect little mourner stares back from the mirror, with clean hair, depressing clothes, and low-heeled shoes. Got to do something about the bags under my eyes.

Teri changed hours ago. According to Toby, she climbed up to the bell tower of the church and has been working her way through a pack of cigarettes. Shock is hardening her into something metallic and permanent.

Over in the church, Betty starts playing the organ.

Funerals are an occupational hazard in a minister's house. I grab a thick black sweater and button it up.

Mikey's casket is the size of a small toy chest. It's closed, thank God. Teri folded his favorite blanket and set it on the foot end. She taped some of his drawings to the sides. The casket rests in front of the altar, a wooden island in a sea of outrageous flowers: roses, hyacinths, tulips, carnations, daffodils, lilies, mums. There has never been so much color in this church before. It makes my nose think of jazz in Central Park.

As people walk in and take their seats, Betty plays *Sesame Street* tunes on the organ, which is a first for this church. Teri insisted. Betty was worried that it wasn't quite holy enough or something. But this morning she said Jesus came to her when she was watching a quilting show on channel 17 and said He's a big *Sesame Street* fan, and that she should play with joy.

Toby and I sit near the front. Mitchell, Sara, and Travis join us. Mitch is decked out in a suit and tie, his shoes shined. Travis put on corduroys and a button-down shirt with a tie. I had no idea that he owned a tie. Sarah is wearing a red top and a long, twirly skirt that has little mirrors sewn into it. She doesn't believe in wearing black to funerals. She gives me a hug before she sits down. People keep coming, more people than I would have thought. The entire hardhat crew is here, all the kitchen ladies, the ambulance drivers, our principal, and a couple of teachers from the vo-tech and preschool, and the librarian.

Teri walks her mother down the center aisle with some help from Ms. Cummings. They sit in the pew in front of us. All of us—Toby, me, Mitch, Sara, and Travis—reach forward one by one and pat Teri's shoulder. She doesn't move.

Betty changes to a dirge. No more *Sesame Street*. We stand and try to sing. Dad isn't even mouthing the words. When the last minor chord warbles away, we sit. Dad takes his place in the pulpit and bows his head. In this light, there is more white in his hair than brown.

One minute ticks by.

He's staring straight down at the closed Bible in front of him. Two minutes. My hands curl into fists, the nails biting the palms. People shift in their seats, bulletins flutter, throats clear. Dad doesn't move. Three minutes pass. Quiet muttering starts in the back of the church. Choir members nudge one another through their gowns. Their pointy elbows look like baby wings.

Dad raises his head. His slack face is streaming with tears.

The conversations stop.

Sara pokes me. "Is he okay?" she whispers.

"Maybe you should do something," Toby says.

Cripes.

"Something could be wrong," Sara says. "Help him."

Just then, Dad pulls a white handkerchief from under his

black robe and blows his nose loudly. When he tucks the handkerchief away, he forces a smile. "Sometimes even your pastor can't find the right words," he says. "If you will open your hymnals . . . "

Dad is back on track. The adults in the congregation sigh and spring into action. They fumble a bit with their hymnals, looking for the right pages. Toby takes my fists out of my lap and loosens my fingers. The service rolls on: a prayer, a hymn, more prayers, a sermon. It's like a stage play, with Dad as the leading man. I try to think of the casket as a prop, but it's useless. Every time I look at it, my stomach flips over.

After half an hour of religion, it's time to wind things up with a closing hymn. Teri chose "Rubber Ducky." I can't get the words out.

## II.I ▌ Beta Decay

TV news cameras have set up across the street. They film the mourners crossing the driveway that separates the church from the graveyard. They focus on Dad and Mr. Lockheart carrying the casket, zoom in on Mrs. Litch leaning on Teri's arm, on Teri's frozen face, the run in her stockings, her work boots and flowered dress. Look at the stupid, poor people. Look at the stupid, poor, burned-out people. Look at the stupid people, poor people, burned-out people, look at their dead baby. It's death porn for the masses.

Dad and Mr. Lockheart set the casket down next to a

small hole dug in the ground. Mikey's grave is in the back corner of the cemetery, uphill from the Litches' house. (He and Mr. Lockheart will lower it into the grave later. People don't like to watch that part.) Betty helps Teri guide Mrs. Litch to the folding chairs lined up by the grave. The rest of the crowd tiptoe in and stand with their heads bowed. My friends and my brother join them. I can't. I stay outside the gate, my back to the cameras. I flex my fingers, try to get some circulation going. Even though the sun is shining, it's freezing today.

Dad opens the faded book and speaks the old words. As he reads, Teri puts her head in her hands and sobs. Dad has to speak louder to be heard. A cardinal lands on my mother's tombstone and chirps, looking for lunch or a mate. Dad can't see it from where he's standing. I have to study the pebbles under my feet and breathe through my mouth. I do not understand death. It is a physical law that energy is neither created nor destroyed. So what happens when people die?

The wind picks up and more birds fly overhead. Teri keeps crying. Dad's voice cracks once. He pauses to rub the back of his neck with his left hand. Other people are sniffing, wiping their eyes. Travis and Sara have their arms around each other, her head on his shoulder. There is still a bit of yellow paint behind his ear. He hides his face in her hair. Mitchell has his hands clasped behind his back. Toby is sitting on the ground plucking grass. Dad's voice deepens, calling on God, spirits big and small. Mikey is, Mikey was, Mikey will be nevermore. Dust.

I walk around to the front of the house and open the door. Somebody has to start the coffee and get the napkins out.

After the funeral, the mourners invade our house armed with casseroles and sympathy cards. Dad greets them at the door. After a quick handshake, they move to the living room to pay their respects. Mrs. Litch sits on the couch, flanked by Betty and Ms. Cummings, the three of them holding cups of black coffee jittering on china saucers. Respects are paid— "I'm sorry, I'm so sorry, we're so sorry for your loss," playing over and over and over again. Mrs. Litch is wearing sunglasses. She nods her head like a queen. Teri is nowhere to be seen. Betty tells people that "she's resting, poor dear."

Part of our church's funeral ritual is to stuff your face. The dining room table is buried under cakes, plates of sandwiches, chips, dips, and several varieties of tuna casserole. I set up the coffee urn and pitchers of iced tea on a card table. The cakes and cookies are laid out on the sideboard. I buzz around resupplying paper plates, cutting cake, and mopping up spills. I make sure there is enough toilet paper in the bathroom. My flu symptoms seem to have abated. Maybe I ate something that was spoiled, or the lack of sleep caught up with me.

Toby disappears into his room with his Game Boy and Mr. Spock. Teri is gone, too. I'm too busy to worry about them right now. I send my friends back to school, back to normal. We all hug-hug, kiss-kiss. Mitch tries to hold on too long. I squirm away.

The adults mingle and murmur—"I'm so sorry, we're so sorry, have another piece of that nut bread, did you get something to drink, your rosebushes look so healthy, what are they going to do, is it true what I heard, apple doesn't fall far from the tree . . . is that a new dress?"—blah, blah, blah. Nobody talks to me, which is fine. The cat raids the ham platter and I stick her in the basement.

And then they leave. Betty and Mrs. Litch are the first to go, then the choir, then one by one the house empties, the cars fill up, and they drive away. Dad has changed out of his robe and into jeans and a sweatshirt. He mutters something and walks back over to the church. I bet he's going to take a nap on the sofa in his office. I wash the dishes. It's my house, after all.


Toby joins me in the kitchen once the coast is clear. "They're gone?"

I set a bowl of tuna casserole on the floor for Mr. Spock. "Perfect timing. The show is over."

"Excellent." He cuts a monstrous piece of chocolate cake and takes a quart of milk out of the fridge.

"Use a glass."

He sighs and grabs a cup. "Dad sleeping?"

I spoon ambrosia salad into a plastic container. "Yep."

"What's with all the food?"

"It's for Teri and her mom. I'm going to freeze it. We can take it down to their place once they get the kitchen finished and the electricity fixed."

"Ummm."

While he eats, I pack up the food. Leftover casserole is dumped into plastic containers, the extra ham is wrapped in aluminum foil, sandwiches are wrapped in plastic. I work steadily, the little engine that could. Toby eats another piece of cake. When he's finished, I point to the dishwasher. He licks the plate before putting it in.

"Is this what it was like when Mom died?" he asks.

I open the freezer slowly. "Don't you remember?"

"No."

I stack the containers of casserole one on top of the other in the freezer. "I guess."

Toby hands me a container. "You guess?"

I put the last container in and shut the door. "Those sandwiches had mayonnaise, didn't they? Can't freeze those." I put the bag of quartered sandwiches in the fridge. "You can take some to school if you want."

"The funeral, Kate."

"It was just a funeral. You've seen plenty."

"Was I there?"

"What?"

"I was real little. Did Dad let me go?"

Okay. The dishes are washed and the food is put away, but the counters are filthy. Somebody spilled lemonade and it looks like the top must have come off a saltshaker. I take the Comet out from under the sink.

"Kate?"

"I don't know."

First I wet the surface and wipe up as much salt as I can. Then I sprinkle the Comet on the countertop, squeeze the sponge under hot water, and scrub. "I don't remember."

Toby leans against the refrigerator. "Dad told me that all the grandparents came, and Grandma Stuart was already senile and kept wandering off."

"If Dad told you about it, why are you bugging me?" I rinse out the sponge and scrub some more.

"Because he won't tell me everything."

I use my thumbnail to scrape away something hard and gray stuck in the middle of the counter. It is oatmeal.

"I think he likes to pretend it never happened," Toby adds.

"You got that right." I rinse the sponge again and wipe down the counter. That looks much better. "Help me with the trash."

Toby snaps open a garbage bag and holds it while I lift the smaller bags of trash and dump them in. "How many people were at Mom's funeral? As many as today?"

I spin the garbage bag and fasten a twist-tie around the neck. "There were lots of cars. They had to park in the front yard and way up both sides of the road."

I set the bag by the back door and wash my hands. Then I snap off a square of plastic wrap. The salad needs to be covered.

Toby hops up on the counter. "Did she have an open casket?"

The plastic sticks to itself. "Geesh, Tobe!" I crumple it in a ball and try again. "I don't remember the casket."

"You're lying."

"No, I'm not." I pull the last of the plastic wrap off the roll and stretch it across the bowl. It seals perfectly.

"Did Dad help carry her casket to the grave?"

"It's morbid to obsess about funerals."

"He carried Mikey's casket. Did he help carry Mom's?"

"I honestly don't know."

"Why not?"

"We need more plastic wrap."

"Why not?"

I open the refrigerator door and talk to the skim milk. "Because I wasn't there, okay? You want to know what I remember? I remember running out of the church. I was wearing black patent leather shoes and I ran down the road and I got blisters and I kept running and the blisters popped and I kept running and then my feet were squishy and wet and I kept sliding in those stupid shoes like I was on ice or something. By the time they found me, Mommy was buried in the ground. I didn't see it happen, I don't remember it. okay?"

Toby pushes himself off the counter. "Yeah, okay. Relax. I just wanted to know."

I let the cold air cool me down before I put the salad on the top shelf. "Sometimes not knowing is better."

I close the door a little too hard and the magnets fall off. Toby bends down and helps me. We work silently, putting up his soccer schedule, my track schedule, his honor roll certificate, my high honor roll certificate, the list of emergency telephone numbers, a postcard of the MIT campus, another postcard, an old one, of the periodic table. The last piece of paper is a drawing of Mikey's, an enthusiastic roundish thing entitled *ball*. I let Toby put that one up.

I wash my hands again. "I'm going to the store to get plastic wrap. Want anything?"

He bites his lip. "Maybe you should go to the store later."

"Why would I want to do that?"

"Well, she was in a hurry. I figured she wanted to get away from everyone, you know."

"No, I don't know. Tell me. Who left?"

"Teri. Teri borrowed your car. An hour ago. She said she needed cigarettes."

## II.2 █ Entropy

Good news: She didn't take Bert far.

Bad news: She's swinging a sledgehammer. And yelling.

I sprint down the hill to the Litch house.

More good news, sort of. She's not pulverizing my car, she's attacking the half-renovated kitchen at the back of her house. The back door has been torn from the hinges and the window smashed to bits. Her hair is coated with dust and swinging wild around her face as she wields the sledgehammer, every blow punctuated with a curse. She's in a trance, lost in the action of beating a counter to death, heart pumping, lungs like bellows.

The kitchen looks worse than it did after the fire. The double-insulated windows are shattered, the new drywall has been ripped from the studs, and all but one of the cabinets have been torn out and smashed on the ground. The sink is still hanging from the wall, but the drainpipe under it is missing. She hasn't torn down the roof or ripped up the floor yet, but the way she's going, it's just a matter of time.

Bert is parked dangerously close to the storm. He looks unharmed, though I bet he has a nail or two in his tires. It's a miracle she hasn't hit him with anything, the way she's tossing lumber and tools around. At least she didn't drive him into a bridge abutment.

Teri drops the hammer and kicks the counter fragments out the door to the ground below. Yesterday there were steps leading from the dirt to the kitchen door. They're gone. She picks up a crowbar and inserts it between the last cabinet and the wall. She leans back, veins standing out in her neck, and pushes with her legs, her butt hanging out for leverage. The nails scream, she swears, and the cabinet breaks free and tumbles to the floor. She tosses the crowbar aside and crouches down to pick it up. It's too big for her to get her arms around.

"You want some help with that?" I ask.

She jumps a bit and squints through the former window in my direction. She's still not wearing her glasses.

"No." She takes a length of rope off the floor and ties it around the fallen cabinet.

I climb up into the kitchen. "That's awfully big. You might hurt yourself."

Teri tightens the knot, then wraps the ends of the rope around her fists. She bends her knees deeply and pulls. The cabinet moves slowly, scraping grooves in the new plywood subfloor. She pulls until the cabinet is almost at the doorway, then she moves to the other side and pushes it off with her boot. It lands on the ground with a little *crack*.

"Or maybe not," I say.

Teri takes off her work gloves and lets them fall. She picks up a can of soda from the floor and gulps it down, then wipes her mouth with the back of her hand. "You come down here to stare at me?"

"No. I was looking for my car. You could have asked, you know."

She crumples the can in her fist and flings it into the yard. "You're such an idiot. Here." She takes something out of her pocket. "I used the keys this time."

She tosses them over my shoulder. I don't move. "It's not just the car. I was worried about you."

"I bet you were."

She slips her work gloves back on, picks up the crowbar, and jumps to the ground. She breaks the cabinet into kindling with a few blows, then kicks the pieces.

"Is the party over yet?" she asks.

"Yep. Your mom went back to Betty's house."

"Did she ask where I was?"

"No."

"Typical." She studies the crowbar in her hand for a second, then sets it on Bert's roof and reaches in for the pack of cigarettes on the dashboard. She shakes one out and sticks it between her lips. She shakes another one halfway out and offers it to me.

"No, thanks."

"Suit yourself." She tosses the pack back in the car and lights up.

"I saved the leftovers for you. They're in the freezer."

She inhales deeply and blows smoke at the sky. It floats above her head like a gray ceiling, then dissipates and drifts away.

"People always bring too much," I say.

She removes a flake of tobacco from her tongue and inhales again. The ash at the end of the cigarette is the same color as her face.

I should go. My car is in one piece. It's none of my business if Teri wants to wreck her house. I need to go home and wash the kitchen floor, check my e-mail, call Diana for the chem lab notes. I have to buy plastic wrap. I should go.

Teri flicks the end of the cigarette with her thumb and the ash crumbles. "I dressed him, you know."

"Dressed who?"

"Who do you think?"

Idiot. Moron. "Oh. Sorry. That must have been hard."

Her chin dips down the tiniest bit, then comes back up. "The funeral guy wasn't going to let me do it at first and I got pissed. But your dad talked to him. Then he said it was okay."

"What was he wearing?" I ask.

Teri smiles a little. "Jeans. Sneakers. Mickey Mouse T-shirt."

I shiver. "Did you put on diapers or pull-ups?"

"Pull-ups. So he could be a big boy—" Her voice breaks off.

I step toward her. She blows past me and leaps up to the kitchen, scooping to grab the sledgehammer. She raises it over her head with a roar and slams it into the wall where the cabinet had been attached.

"Teri, no!"

She can't hear me. I can barely hear me. The air fills with her voice, the hammer hitting the walls, dust, wood, plaster flying in all directions. Her face is red and wet, her mouth open. She screams, screams, hits, hits, stops to pant, then brings the sledgehammer up again and lays into the walls, the door frame, anything that she can destroy.

"Please stop. Look, you're bleeding. Come home with me. I'll take you to the doctor, whatever you want."

She stops to look at the blood on her left forearm, gashed by a piece of wood. She turns over the palms of her hands. She didn't put her gloves back on—they must be raw.

"This isn't doing any good," I say. "You're just wrecking your house. Come on."

She picks up the hammer and breaks through the wall that leads to the playroom, then pounds away until there is enough space to step through. She drops the hammer and disappears inside.

It's quiet. I move along the outside of the house until I can see her through the windows. She's studying Mikey's handprints on the wall, and the "art" we added. It looks so stupid from where I'm standing. I hope she doesn't think we were trying to make fun of her and her family, or that we were defacing her house. Mitch was right, that was a stupid thing to do. We didn't belong there.

"Teri?"

A paint can sails through the closed playroom window, spraying glass like a fountain. The lid comes off in midflight and a yellow swath of paint splats on the ground. A few drops land on my shoes. A second can launches through the middle window. I throw my arms over my head and duck. It arcs over me and explodes in the dirt like a blue bomb.

"Stop!"

Teri comes to the window. "What's wrong, Katie, scared?"

"Of course I am. Look, I'm sorry about the wall. We were trying to, I don't know, we were trying to say good-bye to Mikey. I know it's stupid, I'm sorry."

She picks a shard of glass out of the window frame and tosses it at me.

I jump out of the way. "We'll fix it. We'll repaint it for you. Come on, I'll drive you home."

Her red eyes harden. "I *am* home."

I step toward the window. "Exactly. That's my point. This is your house. You can't tear it down."

"Watch me. I'm going to rip out every board, every beam, every door, all the locks, the stairs, the walls, the freaking windows. . . . "

She steps away from the window, then—*smash*—the sledgehammer comes down on the frame, splintering the wood. She whales away at the frame until she can kick the whole thing out of the wall. She stands where the window used to be, struggling to catch her breath. "You can help me or you can go home. Suit yourself."

"Teri, you need professional help. This is not normal."

Her laugh sounds like cloth ripping. "What the hell is normal?"

"You need time to deal with this, talk to a counselor or something."

"That's bull."

"You're not thinking."

"I don't want to think."

"That's ridiculous."

She pulls a broken piece of plaster-covered wood from the wall. "Ridiculous? When I wasn't looking, my kid wandered upstairs and got killed. He had his brains fried. I don't want to think, Kate. Never again."

She turns her face away.

In the distance, there are cars and trucks speeding on the highway. The sound of their tires on the road provides a background hum, background radiation, like the ticking clock or dripping faucet you don't notice until you notice it, and then the sound drives you nuts. My little black dress and my velvet headband feel like they are on a different body, like I'm inhabiting something else, the space between Teri and me, maybe, or maybe I left myself back up the hill. My hands are ice, but Teri is dripping sweat. What does it feel like to drive a sledgehammer through a wall? To scream so loud that the birds fly away? To rip down an entire house because it hurts so much to look at it?

"I'm sorry," my mouth says. "I came down here to help you."

"No, you didn't!" she screams. "You came for your god-damn car! Get out!"

She's not rational. Get a grip, Malone. I pull my sweater closed and tie the belt around my waist. I rub my hands up and down on my arms and clear my throat once. "I wish I could help you."

"Fuck you very much."

Well, then. I pick up the keys and get in my car, which reeks of smoke. I roll down the windows and toss out Teri's pack of cigarettes and the soda. According to the odometer, she only drove eleven miles, but I doubt that she remembered to shift. Probably killed the transmission. Poor Bert. I pat the dashboard and put him in reverse.

A paint can flies through the last intact window of the playroom. The sound of exploding glass makes me flinch and stomp on the gas. Bert shoots backward and the can bounces off the top of the windshield on the passenger side. It tips and pours red paint everywhere.

I slam on the brakes and throw it into park. It takes a few

minutes to stop shaking, a few more to realize that the windshield is still in one piece. The glass has a small spiderweb crack where the can hit, but the rest of the windshield is whole.

Teri stays out of sight, banging and cursing inside. I turn the heat on high and flick on the wipers. The motor whines as the blades smear the thick red paint across the glass. Back and forth. Back and forth. Back and forth.

# 12.0 | Activated Complex

*SAFETY TIP: Never mix chemicals without a defined procedure.*

Dad's mechanic promises to look through some junkyards for me. He swears the crack won't get any bigger as long as I avoid speed bumps and I don't exceed ten miles per hour. Poor Bert. I stick him in the garage to recuperate. After dinner I lose myself on-line. Teri stops by to chat with Dad. By the time I go downstairs for something to drink, she's gone. Dad says that she decided to stay at Betty's house for a while. She'll pick up the rest of her stuff tomorrow.

Fine.

I go out for a little run at midnight. There is a light on upstairs at the Litches'. A flickering candle.

Fine.

After colleges have sent out acceptances and rejections, it's rather pointless to make seniors show up for class. Like they have something new to teach us? Please. But I am still Kate Malone, so I attend class on autopilot. I keep forgetting to do homework, but I'll make it up later. The week plays out without drama. I go through the motions, move from station to station along the assembly line. At night I run, in the morning I sleepwalk. I keep my curtains closed and try not to breathe too much. This flu/not-flu thing has put a big hurt on me.

Teri's name shows up on the absent list daily. Good Kate thinks about collecting her books and homework, but somehow I don't get around to it. I have her clothes, toothbrush, lighter, magazines, all her junk packed in a duffel bag, waiting by the front door. She hasn't stopped by.

It takes Dad a couple of days to figure out that a) Teri is living in her house, and b) Teri is destroying her house. I watch from the sidelines as he moves from concern to deep concern to frustration to anger. He tries to talk to Teri. She treats him the same way she treated me, more or less. He tries to talk to her mom. He talks to the police, two shrinks, county social services, and back again to Mrs. Litch. The answers drive him crazy. She can't be arrested; it's not against the law to knock out walls in your house, not with the water and electricity already turned off. She won't need a demolition permit until she breaks through an outside or retaining wall. She's eighteen years old, so no one can go after her for cutting school. She's living in a house that her family owns, so social services won't get involved. And her mother doesn't care one way or another, as long as she can keep living at Betty's. Basically, Teri is doing what she wants and nobody can stop her.

She'll move out of there eventually; November, maybe. Definitely by the first snow.

Toby has to write a biography about someone for his English class. He wants to write about our mother. I suggest he choose a different subject. He slams his door and turns up his CD so loud it scares the dog.

I sleep all weekend or maybe I don't sleep at all. Hard to tell what is asleep and what is awake. They have blurred into each other. I've given up on my contacts. Wearing them is like jamming thistles in my eyes. My glasses are fine.

In the bottom of Toby's clothes hamper, I come across Mikey's pajamas and one of his socks. It takes me a couple of hours to wash and iron them. I fold and lay them under my pillow.

The last track meet of the season is on Tuesday, a week after the funeral. A big deal, this one. Last chance to qualify for states. Perfect weather. My father and brother in the crowd to watch my final race.

When the starter's gun goes off, I just stand there. My feet refuse to move. Very odd. They have always moved before. I sit down on the starting line. My legs are still attached, knees operational, socks rolled down, shoelaces tied. I stand up. Nope, the feet will not race. It's not dark enough, I guess. Dad drives me home. He wants me to take a nap.

I wake up in the middle of the night. The Litch house is quiet. It's been quiet for three days. I can't tell if that's a good sign or a bad sign. Dad has stopped talking about Teri. To me, at least.

Mitchell e-mails and I delete. He took it upon himself to tell everyone about my little college disaster. Sara has been spending a lot of time in my face, trying to get me to talk about it, to "share." Travis thinks I need a road trip. Mostly I think about the advantages of being abducted by aliens. The pharmacy calls and fires me on the answering machine. Good Kate and Bad Kate have not come home. Either they are lost or I scared them off.

I have a new slant to my Quantum Futures options. I could work in a coal mine. I could move to Australia, learn how to shear sheep. I could donate my body and brain to science. I could volunteer at a Third World orphanage. I could work on a cutter in the Arctic. When I show Sara the new list, she throws it out.

On Thursday, Ms. Cummings catches me mixing Dangerous Chemical A with Dangerous Chemical B in class. This creates quite a reaction. We have to evacuate the building, which is a pain.

On Friday, Dad makes me stay home and commands me to rest. As if. When he leaves, I sneak into Toby's room to clean. I open the windows, strip the bed, take out the trash, and put all of his gym socks in a caustic bleach bath. His Mom project is on his desk, hidden under a layer of comic books and algebra notes. He has glued photos and written down a few facts: born on . . . went to college . . . married . . . taught math . . . died on. . . . Hobbies: fractals, studying transition metals, knitting. He didn't write down that her favorite perfume smelled like roses. Or that she knew the value of pi to the fortieth digit. Or that she knew all of Tom Lehrer's songs. Or that she used to stay up with Toby all night to make sure he kept breathing. Or that she liked a clean kitchen. Or that she was Phi Beta Kappa at MIT. Maybe she called it Pi Beta Kappa.

And then I am in bed quite sure that I am awake, and then I'm running, convinced that I'm asleep. I have a dream in which Mitchell "Lips" Pangborn tells me none of this would have happened if I had learned to write better essays. And then he puts me on hold while he talks to some chick in Cambridge.

I can't get warm. I pile all the blankets from the linen closet on my bed, and my winter coat, and a sleeping bag, too. I put my head under the covers, worry for a second about the possibility of a carbon dioxide/oxygen imbalance, then crash.

# 13.0 | Critical Pressure

*SAFETY TIP: Do not use reflected sunlight for microscope illumination.*

When I wake up, it is Saturday and Sara is standing over me, frowning her displeased goddess frown. "Okay, that's enough. Get out of bed and take a shower. You're coming with me."

It would take too much energy to argue with her. I do as I'm told. Once I'm clean and dressed, I follow her outside. She sends me back inside with instructions to put in my contacts and comb my hair. I do as I'm told, then return. Travis is driving. I get in the back seat. Sara tells me to buckle up.

We drive across town to the Salt City Diner. I am just barely in the car, an essence of Kate. Good thing I put the belt on. Up front, Sara fiddles with the radio, twirls her hair around her finger and talks a mile a minute. It takes a while, but eventually I can hear what she's saying. Nonsense, most of it, but it is sweet of her to try.

The diner is a grown-up version of the Merryweather cafeteria, except the food tastes better and costs less. Nine o'clock on a Saturday morning is rush hour here. Families with screaming babies are all seated in the back. Divorced dads starting their custody weekends with pissed-off kids sit by the windows. The booths are mostly taken by teenagers, the tables in the middle of the floor are for adults—both groups armed and ready for serious gossip. The old people have already cleared out. Waitresses with hideous orange aprons move like skaters between the kitchen and the tables. Eating here is like trying to eat inside a pinball game, but Sara thinks the place has atmosphere.

Mitchell is already in a booth, waiting for us. He slides down the bench to make room for me and pours the coffee. "You're alive," he says. "I was beginning to wonder."

Travis and Sara lean forward a little, their eyes intent on me.

I sigh and open my menu. "You guys can knock it off. I know what you're doing. I'm fine. I had some weird flu, but I slept like a log last night, and I'm starving. What are you going to eat?"

Sara grins and wriggles in her seat. "You're back. Oh, sweetie, I was so worried."

Travis pulls his wallet out of his back pocket and extracts three dollars. "Tell me, O Brilliant Mistress: What is the maximum amount of food I can get for this?"

"Are you talking number of bites or weight?" I ask.

"Weight. I want it to feel it."

"Then you want oatmeal," I say. "It's like cement."

Mitch shakes his head. "Wrong again, Malone. Our boy needs pancakes to fill him up."

"Duh. How do you make pancakes? It's chemistry; you

combine baking powder with an acid like sour milk. The reaction creates air bubbles, which make the pancakes fluffy. Fluffy is not filling. Plus the pancakes cost twice as much as the oatmeal."

"They taste better," Mitch says.

"He wants weight, not taste. If he wants taste, he could order cherry pie."

"We're not talking about pie."

"I'm not talking about pie, either, alls I'm saying is—"

"I don't want to argue, Kate."

"I'm not arguing."

Sara reaches her hand across the table and gently pats my arm. "No, sweetie, but you're yelling, and a little vein on the side of your forehead just popped out. Do you want some decaf?"

The three of them stare at me. No, I will not touch the vein. I won't give them the satisfaction. "I'm fine. Pass the cream and the fake sugar."

Travis passes over the goodies. Mitchell waves his hand in the air, trying to attract the attention of the waitresses clustered around the coffee machines. The oldest waitress, whose hair was lacquered into place in the mid-sixties, shouts into the kitchen. A new waitress strolls out. She's wearing work boots and has a pack of cigarettes sticking out of the pocket of her apron. She's wearing her hospital bracelet and my watch and my gold necklace with the heart on it. She has a scabby "M" tattooed on her forearm. Theresa Litch, decorated in a waitress-orange apron, walks to our table.

Crapcrapcrap. I knew I should have stayed home.

She stops at our booth, hands on her hips. "Yeah?"

"What happened to the other waitress?" Mitch asks. "The one who brought the coffee?"

"I pushed her in the lake. You gonna order or what?"

"Yes. Yes, we're ready to order," Sara says. "Hi, Teri. I'm having crêpes with strawberries, extra whipped cream. Please."

Travis opens his menu again. "What'll fill me up more, pancakes or oatmeal?"

"Pancakes," Teri says. "They're like lead."

"They're not fluffy?"

"Hockey pucks."

Travis winks at me. "Perfect. Give me a tall stack, extra syrup."

"What about you, Harvard?" she asks Mitch.

"Aren't you going to write any of this down?" he asks.

"Because it's so complicated, right?"

Mitch taps his finger on the table for a second, then gives in. "Three eggs, sunny-side up, bacon—not overcooked, I like it soft and greasy. Wheat toast, no butter, large orange juice, and a bowl of fruit. Oh, and we need more coffee." He slides the empty pot down the table.

"What about you, Katie?"

I keep my eyes on the table in front of me. I could be home ironing. I could be giving the dog a bath. I could be changing Bert's oil. I could be researching state colleges. I could be shaving the cat. . . . "Just bring me a doughnut. A glazed doughnut. And more water."

Teri snorts once and walks back to the kitchen.

Sara leans across the table. "Did you know she was working here?"

I shake my head. "Last I knew she was working at some bar."

Travis puts his arm around Sara. "What's the story with her house? Is she still tearing it down?"

"Who knows? She won't talk to anyone, won't let anyone near the place. And her mom is looney tunes. She might end up in a home. I don't know. I mean, look, you just can't help Teri."

"That's harsh," Travis says.

"So's Teri," Mitch says.

Sara throws her napkin at him. "Be nice. Would you like to be in her shoes?"

"Her boots," I say. "She won't wear shoes. Only boots." I take Sara's napkin from Mitch and smooth it out on the tabletop with the palm of my hand. "She's going to get blood poisoning from that tattoo, septicemia."

"No, she won't." Travis pulls up his shirt and points to the yin yang symbol tattooed on the middle of his stomach. "I did that one myself. I didn't get sick."

"I've been thinking about getting a tattoo," Mitchell says.

I shake my head. "It'll hurt your chances of getting into grad school."

"Really?"

Travis throws his napkin at Mitch. "Don't be such a tool."

It only takes a few minutes for Teri to deliver our order. She slams the plates on the table and tosses the silverware in the middle. Travis spreads the butter on his pancakes. Mitchell unfolds his napkin in his lap and loads his eggs with salt. Sara dips her pinkie finger into the strawberry gunk drooling out of her crêpes.

I stare at my plate: two pieces of dried bread.

"Everything all right?" Teri asks.

"I ordered a glazed doughnut, not toast," I say. "And we need coffee. And I need water. I'm thirsty. "

Sara goes bug-eyed, trying to get me to back down, as if that is going to make Teri's life any easier. Or mine.

"The doughnuts are all stale."

"I doubt that."

Teri takes my toast plate and stomps away. She returns with a glazed doughnut and a pot of fresh coffee. The doughnut has a thumbprint mashed into it.

"I didn't spit on it, if that's what you're thinking," Teri says. She stands there, arms crossed over her chest for a minute. I half expect her to pick up the table and fling it through the front window. Instead, she sits down.

"Move over, skinny," she says. Sara scootches closer to Travis and Teri slides in next to her. "So, what's up, kids? Are we having fun? Making big plans for the prom?"

Travis mumbles something through a mouthful of pancakes. Mitchell punctures his yolk with the corner of his toast and yellow floods his plate.

"We haven't decided yet," Sara says to Teri, as if this were a remotely normal conversation. "Are you going?"

Teri takes my spoon and bends the handle. "You're joking, right?"

Sara stuffs half a crêpe in her mouth to save herself from answering. I carefully break out the thumbprint from my doughnut, and take a bite of the unthumbed part. It's stale, all right. A week old, at least.

"Hey, Teri!" yells the ancient waitress. "Back to work."

"I'm on break," she yells back. She holds her arm up and points to my watch. "I get five minutes."

"Are you going to sell your house?" Mitch asks.

Teri wags the bent spoon at him. "Why do you care?"

He has yolk on his chin. "My mom's an agent. It could be nice if you fix it up, but you'd get a lot more if you sold it. It's a big piece of property. Somebody could put up condos."

Teri takes a piece of his bacon. "I've been thinking about it."

"Yeah, I bet you have," I say. "I asked for some water."

"Keep your panties on. You know jack about what I'm thinking."

"I know precisely what you're thinking."

Teri snorts and reaches for my doughnut. Mitch's hand shoots across the table and grabs her wrist. I wasn't planning on him doing that. And then his voice sounding like it crawled out from under a rock: "Don't touch her food," he says.

"Chill, Pangborn," Travis says.

Teri's eyes go flat behind the thick lenses of her glasses. Her fingers collect into a fist. "What are you going to do about it, Harvard?"

Mitch leans toward her and squeezes harder. "I don't have to do anything. You did it yourself. We're all really sorry that Mikey was killed, and I know you've had a really hard life. But that doesn't give you permission to make Kate feel like shit, or make fun of people, or steal from them. Don't touch her food."

He releases her wrist and sits back. His fingernails made red half-moons in her skin.

"Break's over," calls the old waitress.

Teri blinks a few times, breathing hard. Her arm is still lying across the table—fist, red fingernail marks, snaky blue veins, crooked tattoo.

"Kate asked for water," Mitch says as he spears his egg.

She stands up. Her apron is wrinkled. "She's got plenty."

"I mean it, Litch!" the old waitress hollers.

Teri reaches behind her and tugs at the bow in her apron strings until it comes undone. She walks away from our booth, pulling the apron over her head as she goes.

"Oh, no," Sara whispers.

"Way to go, Pangborn," Travis says. "That was bone-headed."

"It's not my fault if she quits. Another day and they would have fired her."

They won't look at me. Sara and Travis dig into their

food. Mitchell pours himself another cup of coffee. Over the noise of the crying babies, buzzing conversations, and forks scraping plates, tapping spoons on mugs, I can hear shouting in the kitchen. I could have stayed home and avoided all of this. I could have scrubbed the toilets, cleaned grout.

Teri bursts through the kitchen doors. She makes for the front door, then stops, pivots on her left boot, and marches back to our table. She stands over me. The diner has gone quiet all of a sudden. I can smell her. Out of the corner of my eye, I can see her hands balled up and ready to inflict pain. Should I apologize for what the jerk to my left said? Should I do that before or after she breaks his jaw?

Teri opens her fist and drops my gold necklace on the table. She unbuckles my watch and sets it carefully next to the water glass. She is still wearing her hospital bracelet.

When she walks out the door, the diner sighs and the noise cranks back up to full volume: crying, buzzing, scraping, tapping.

Sara reaches for the coffeepot. "That was nice of her."

Mitch frowns. "You gave her my necklace?"

I pick up the watch. The band is damp with sweat. She poked an extra hole in it so she could buckle it. I wrap the band around my wrist and buckle it in her hole. Her sweat is clammy and slick. The watch flops around my wrist, the weight of the face pulling it down.

"I can't believe that fit her," Travis says. "She's, like, twice as big as you are."

Mitch tilts his head to one side. "Why did you give her my necklace?"

I pick up the part of the doughnut that has Teri's thumbprint and stick it in my mouth. It's dry as a rock and just as hard. I take a swig of coffee and hold it in my mouth until the doughnut softens, then turns to mush. My friends talk over and around me, prom blah-blah, work blah-blah, the lake blah-blah, summer blah, September, financial aid blah-blah-blah. I'm shrinking and they don't even notice. . . .

My watch is ticking, but the second hand isn't moving. I breathe quickly, deeply, like I'm sprinting, even though I am sitting down. I blink, trying to moisten my contacts. As I open my eyes, it's like I'm rocketing through space, the stars elongating past me as, sitting still, I shift into warp drive and break the speed of light.

Someone mentions MIT, but it doesn't save me. Sara blows bubbles in her coffee with a straw. The bubbles pop and more words come out . . . admissions, transfer, room-mates, GPAs, microwaves, concerts, registration. God, is this all we ever talk about?

The diner air is jelling, concentrating, molecules collapsing into the void, the invisible gases taking shape and mass. I hold my water glass up to my nose. Seen through the water, the faces and bodies around me flatten under an unseen weight. I don't recognize anyone.

I hold the glass of water over the aisle so it can catch the morning light. The water acts as a prism, creating a rainbow that cascades across the table. The glare surprises Mitch and he puts his hand up to shield his face.

Water is an extremely efficient solvent: two atoms of hydrogen connected to one atom of oxygen by highly polar covalent bonds. Given enough time, it can dissolve almost anything, even sunlight into pure color. The electrolysis of water is a classic chemistry experiment. Stick two electrodes in water, add a bit of electrolytic solution, and turn on the battery. *Voilà.* Hydrogen collects at the cathode, oxygen collects at the anode. It's not water anymore, not even steam. Bonds are broken and the substance is reduced to its elements. Magic.

"Are you all right?" Sara asks me.

I open my fingers.

The glass falls.

Gravity works.

It lands on the tile floor without a sound, shattering into a dozen shards and countless diamond slivers. The tidal wave of water washes over me, and I have to close my mouth so I don't breathe it into my lungs. I am at sea. There are ghosts in these waters, aliens, and lost little blonde girls, all waiting for me to open my eyes. They have been waiting a long time.

The wave crests and rushes past me. I emerge soaked to the skin and shaking. My friends have stopped talking. They aren't eating either. Mitchell reaches out and wipes the tears from my face. His hand smells like bacon.

"What's wrong?" he asks.

# 13.1 ▌ Covalent Bonding

If I could run all the time, life would be fine. As long as I keep moving, I'm in control. She wasn't in the parking lot. I haven't passed her walking on the road, either. There's no way she's running, too. Not Teri. She could have hot-wired a car, I guess, but it's more likely she hitchhiked. Somebody must have picked her up. No matter. I know where she's headed. East. Home. She doesn't have anywhere else to go.

Stepstepstepstep . . . breathe, breathe. Stepstepstepstep . . . breathe, breathe. Jeans and a sweatshirt are not exactly recommended running gear. No matter. It feels good to run in the sun. I'm warming up. Teri's watch swirls around my wrist, my heart bounces against the wet skin between my breasts.

From the road, the Litch house looks abandoned. Some of the windows are open, others closed. The shutters that had been taken down for sanding and painting are still stacked against the maple tree. There is trash scattered in the yard. Pink and yellow tufts of insulation are tangled in the bushes. They look like clown wigs.

My heart is pounding as I walk up the driveway. How many miles was that? A thousand, maybe. More. In a sweatshirt and jeans, imagine that.

The dirty bulb in the porch light is broken. The thin glass shards litter the floor of the porch. The side door is open, but the house is silent. I cross the threshold.

"Teri?"

The living room is packed again, jammed with all the

furniture from the other rooms. The wood floor is covered in dust and footprints. Mikey's corner is empty.

"Teri?"

All that's left of the kitchen is a shell. She even took out the sink. She ripped out the wall between the kitchen and the playroom. The holes that used to be playroom windows gape open. Tools are lined up in a neat row on the floor. Her tool belt, too. The wall with Mikey's handprints and our feeble cave art is untouched.

I walk back down the hall and climb the stairs. The new railing is still in place. The walls in the upstairs hall have fist-sized holes in them.

"Teri?"

I find her sitting in the middle of the floor in Mikey's room, her head leaning against her knees, her arms wrapped around her head. There's a pile of blankets in the corner, a couple of bottles of soda, potato chip and pretzel bags, two apples.

"I'd like to talk to you," I say. "Please."

She lifts her right hand and gives me the finger.

I sit down, cross-legged, three feet in front of her. "I don't blame you. But I'm not leaving."

She lifts her left hand and gives me another finger.

"I can wait," I say.

She lowers her hands and wraps them around her head again.

I take off my watch and set it on the floor between us. The ticking fills the room, swaying the curtains back and forth. The tidal wave builds again. I don't flinch. I don't even hold my breath. I let it wash over me.

Teri reaches out and pulls the watch to her side. Another minute passes, then she lifts her head and tucks her hair behind her ears. Her face is tearstained, her eyes swollen and red. She leaves the watch on the ground.

"What's wrong with your face?" she asks. "It looks like a fat zit ready to pop."

"Thanks."

The watch keeps ticking. Can't she hear it?

"And you're crying," she says. "You never cry."

"Imagine that," I whisper. I sniff and clear my throat. "I'm sorry for what Mitch did, what he said. That was wrong, worse than wrong, it was disrespectful and you didn't deserve it."

"He's your boyfriend."

"Not really. But I don't want to talk about him anymore. We need to talk about Mikey, about what happened."

"No, we don't." Teri leans back, puts her arms behind her, and stretches out her legs until her boots are right in front of me. "I heard you looking around downstairs. I haven't gotten much done."

"Kitchen looks nice."

She manages a chuckle. "Yeah. I wanted to get that out of the way first."

I wipe my eyes on my sleeve. "I like the way you made the kitchen open to the playroom."

She rocks her boots from side to side. "I had it all planned, you know. I could be cooking and he could be in the playroom, and that way we could see each other. Lots of houses are built that way these days."

"It's a really good idea."

"Waste of time." Her boots are like a metronome, back and forth, back and forth.

"No, it's not. You still need a place to live; so does your mom."

Back and forth, back and forth. "You said you were sorry. You can go now."

I grab her boots and hold them still. "Will you stop that?"

She stands up, rises above me, puts her fists on her hips. "You got something to say to me?"

Her movement sends a thousand motes of dust spinning in the sunlight coming through the window. Our essence is in this room, the atomic products of breaking down two girls to their elemental selves; frightened, defiant, lonely. I can hear the glass breaking over and over again, piercing the frozen tissue around my heart.

I look up at her. "Do you think it was your fault that he died? Or my fault? Dad's fault?"

She turns her face quickly, but not fast enough. The tidal wave caught her, too, and we're both crying. She sniffs hard and wipes her nose on her shirt.

"No," she whispers.

"Are you sure?"

She nods, and wipes her eyes. "That's the worst part. It was nobody's fault really, or it was everyone's fault. It was an accident, just one damn accident after another."

"Your father. What he did wasn't an accident. It was a crime."

She nods again. "He paid."

I start to stand. Teri reaches down a hand and helps me up. I dig a tissue out of my purse and give it to her.

"You're always prepared, aren't you? What were you, a freaking Brownie?"

"Girl Scout."

"That's right. You had that stupid hat." She blows her nose.

"You filled that hat with yellow snow."

"Did I? Sorry."

We're standing eye to eye. I never think of Teri as my height. In my mind, she's at least six foot five. But in real life, we're the same size, except for her fifty pounds of muscle. I can't hear the watch ticking anymore. I pick it up. It's running fine, it's just back to telling time quietly.

"Here." I hand it to her. "I want you to have this. It fits you better. But I'm keeping the necklace."

"You should sell it, get some cash."

"I might."

"Thanks." She buckles it on her wrist and checks the time.

The dust between us has settled and the light is coming through the window at a higher angle.

"You promised that you would would teach me how to hammer," I say.

"You're a spaz; it's impossible."

"I'd like to try again. I'd like to help you put the house back together."

She adjusts the band on her wrist. "What, you mean this summer, before you go off to be Einstein?"

I look around the room. "I was thinking of staying until the job is finished."

"For real?"

I nod.

"You're full of it. You're going to college."

"Not right away. I'm taking some time off. I've been running too much. My legs need a rest."

She studies me for a minute, then walks out of the room. I follow her down the stairs and across the porch. I follow her all the way to the bottom of the hill. She looks at my house and then at hers.

"You can't slack if you're going to work with me."

"I won't. I promise."

She brings her face close to mine, closer than she has ever been. Magnified by her glasses, her eyes are impossibly large, taking in every detail.

Finally she leans back and pushes up her sleeves. "When do you want to start?"

"Now."

# Acknowledgments

The idea that authors write alone is bogus. I sure don't. Here are the people and things that served as catalysts for the writing of this book:

The family: My daughters, Meredith and Stephanie, get all the credit in the world for giving me the time and mental space I needed for this one. (And no, this story is not about either one of them.) Thank you for your patience and for loving me enough to let me journey after my heart, even when the path was bumpy. Thanks also to Greg for friendship, freedom, and comma editing. I promise to join a support group for Semicolon Addicts; any day now. And Mom and Dad—you were right. I did finish it, after all. How come you're always right?

The editors: Sharyn November, who was my sister in another life, and Regina Hayes, who was our aunt. I don't have enough words to thank you for your amazing support and encouragement. Thanks to Catherine Frank, whose comments brought Kate to life.

The friends: The Bucks County Children's Writers Group sparks my imagination and determination every month. Special thanks to Deb Heiligman for our writing mornings, and Joyce McDonald and Martha Hewson for e-encouragement.

I face the West Coast and bow deeply in gratitude to Betsy Partridge, who allowed me to spend an intense week of writing at the Partridge Family Coop with a handful of other writers. Thank you to all for not talking to me when I had that glazed look in my eyes. Betsy gets a second shout-out along with Susan Campbell Bartoletti for helping me with the concept of long-term planning. Elizabeth Mikesell told me I wasn't crazy when I most needed to hear it (always a valuable ability in a friend). Dan Darigan was my favorite cheerleader. And Scot Larrabee . . . Scot was the surprise element at the end of a long and complicated reaction. Chemistry, indeed . . .

The experts: Alvin C. Lavoie, Ph.D. and Serious Chemistry Guy, read the manuscript in draft and kept me from falling on my face. I came perilously close to flunking chemistry in high school, so if there are any science mistakes in the book, they are my fault, not his. Always wear your safety goggles, class. Also, many thanks to Janine Ricci for saving my butt with some much-needed cross-country information.

The agent: Amy Berkower of Writers House, who also belongs in the paragraph about friends. Thank you so much for taking care of business.

The rest of the world: Thanks to my eighth-grade English teacher for introducing me to Greek mythology, many thanks to Beethoven, Y100 in Philadelphia, Incubus, Dave Matthews, Tori Amos, Staind, Count Basie Orchestra, Santana, Linkin Park, the Doobie Brothers, Sting, Mozart, and the baristas at the Maple Glen Starbucks. Make mine a venti.

**Laurie Halse Anderson**, herself a minister's daughter and runner, is the author of the award-winning novels *Speak* and *Fever 1793*, as well as five picture books. She has two teenage daughters and lives just outside of Philadelphia, Pennsylvania.

Visit her Web site at **www.writerlady.com**